SAINTS

OF

THE

HOUSE
HOLD

SAINTS
OF
THE

HOUSE
HOLD

ARI TISON

FARRAR STRAUS GIROUX
NEW YORK

Farrar Straus Giroux Books for Young Readers
An imprint of Macmillan Publishing Group, LLC
120 Broadway, New York, NY 10271 • mackids.com

Our books may be purchased in bulk for promotional, educational, or business use. Please
contact your local bookseller or the Macmillan Corporate and Premium Sales Department at
(800) 221-7945, ext. 5442, or by email at MacmillanSpecialMarkets@macmillan.com.

Library of Congress Cataloging-in-Publication Data is available.

First edition, 2023
Book design by L. Whitt
Printed in the United States of America

Special thanks to the reader who considered the representation of Anishinaabe
culture and characters in this novel and provided invaluable feedback.

ISBN 978-0-374-38949-9 (hardcover)

1 3 5 7 9 10 8 6 4 2

TO THE ONE ABOVE,
TO THOSE BEFORE,
TO THOSE AHEAD,
TO THOSE WHO ARE NOW

SAINTS

OF

THE

HOUSE
HOLD

I

JAY

COMMUNION

We hold deep dark cups, dark like the cloth they bring out on Maundy Thursday to place over the cross and the tables at Hope Oak Church. I keep crying at the time of reflection, asking God for forgiveness (for kicking the neighbor's dog, for shouting at the sky, for beating up *that boy*, and maybe even worse, for hurting Nicole). I can't stop thinking about it—before I am told to eat the cracker and drink the two-inch cup of black-red wine.

Hold the cup tight enough and you can see your heart beating in the surface even when you doubt it's there.

FIRST DAY BACK

People try not to look at us in the hallway. After we'd been suspended for two weeks, our classmates scatter like we might swallow them. Us, these angry brown boys ready to snap. What does it mean when we scare everyone—the good and the bad?

Maybe someday I will walk down the hall, and someone will see the human in me. It won't be just Mom, God, and Max. Is Nicole in that group? I haven't seen her since the woods, only DMing her my apologies. No response.

Max follows close behind, his coyote eyes averting, and I feel all my pull-ups bulk in my shoulders, my stomach, and in the veins that plump thick down my forearms. I keep my chin up. Keep my lips tight, and I am grateful that we are taller than most. This way, I can't see their eyes, their fear of us. This way, I am not tempted to want more.

NICOLE

I go through the day without seeing her. Nicole and us, we are cousins, the complicated kind, but cousins nonetheless. She's my father's stepniece; her mother is his stepsister. Before Nicole's parents divorced in fifth grade, she grew up just a few miles from us. She went to the same schools, and we were friend-cousins in class, inseparable, and family-cousins on holidays. She, her mom, her dad, her sister—Tia—were the only Native family we have on our dad's side. She, her sister, and her mom enrolled at the Red Lake Nation. Dad's side entwined by marriage.

Tia is a clothing and jewelry designer studying in New Mexico. She was the one to smooth-talk all the adults, the one with the coolest clothes, wearing designer brands she'd revamp from the steals she'd find at thrift stores or save up for at the mall. But Nicole has always been book brilliant. She'd be the first one to teach us something new. Psychology, herbology, ecology. The cousin who would take some distant relative's baby in her arms and show us their reflexes. A finger for their hands to clasp, a graze to the cheek and they'd get all wide-eyed and hungry. I wonder if she somehow knows what everyone thinks. I know she now studies the mind, reactions, attachments, and misplacements. What did she learn about Max and me from that day in the woods? My stomach turns.

But she's always had empathy—even for the bullies. Befriended most people at school. And I remember how Nicole cared for herself, too, making meals, doing her own laundry. Meanwhile, Max and I were just figuring out how often to shower.

Grandpa taught us to respect our relatives here and to know whose land we are on. The ever and always truth is that we, all of us, are on Anishinaabe land here in northeastern Minnesota. We are all on Nicole's land.

COUNSELING

Max and I have our first meeting with the school counselor after our last classes. Ms. Hannan schedules us to meet with her together once a week after school, and closes her black calendar book. She wastes no time. She has us practice deep breathing, visualizing the ocean—a beach—what she calls our "safe place." I smile and sense Max smirking through his breathing patterns. We know our people aren't beach people no matter what our counselor might assume about Costa Rica. To us, the ocean is a fierce woman, and if we were there, traditionally, we'd have to pray to even get close. With Ms. Hannan, we try cognitive therapy, re-scaping our minds with warmer thoughts so we can prepare to talk to Luca for "reconciliation." Our first session with Luca is tomorrow. After we do this, she asks us questions that start kind but build to:

> *Why didn't you stop? Why did you kick him in the face? You broke his nose.*

Which one of us broke his nose? Do we even remember?

> *His face is severely injured.*

What can we say? We are sorry; we will never do it again?

> *We are angry*, we finally say. This is true.

> *But we don't know why.* This is not true.

WALK HOME

With hands on our backpack straps, we laugh at the small, ratty dog barking at us from a house window. The little dog fogs up the glass against the late January cold. Max and I take turns kicking a pebble before he picks it up and notes the rust colors aloud. *Spice. Marigold. Fire.*

Okay, show-off, I tease. Before winter break, before all this with Nicole and Luca, Max was letting himself love art even more. Though he's never shown me much, he decided lately he wanted to go to art school. He's gone from his sketchbook to full-blown paintings prepping for his application to Minneapolis College of Art and Design. Their last April deadline is his goal, a fall start. He puts the pebble in his pocket.

What I don't say is that this walk home is what I imagine a good life would be before death. You know something terrible is going to get you in the end, but you act like you don't know that most of the time. We talk about how everyone sucks in high school. How no one greeted us back today. Not even the people I study calculus with. None of Max's new art friends. How neither of us saw Nicole. How there are only five months left of high school anyway, so why should anything matter? I look at my phone. It's five fifteen. I tell Max.

We start walking faster.

POTATOES

We find Mom cutting potatoes in the kitchen. Hard-bodied tubers, first sliced in half—the way she plants them in the spring—their white exposed and then placed in the ground, a white face to a brown one. Then she scores them into half circles to bake.

Potatoes grow well here, and she keeps them in her pantry so we have them throughout the winter, when we're stuck inside for months. If we lived in Costa Rica, with all of Mom's extended family, I think she would prefer to be outside every day in a garden. Every day bringing in something new. Instead, the lack of sun is harder on us, whose bodies belong in the warmth and light. Despite Dad's Nordic genes, he seems to be upset at all times of the year.

Mom gives Max and me kisses on the cheeks, saying, "Mijos, how was your first day back?"

We say, "Fine." Like before. But I can tell we are both relieved that we got here first. We are back to our after-school routine, but now with a tighter turnaround on counseling days. Somehow we all managed to hide our suspension from Dad. Mom had us go to the Central Park Recreational Center to do our community service after winter break for two weeks before we were allowed to go back. I don't even want to imagine what would have happened if Dad knew.

NEIGHBOR'S DOG

I take the trash out while Max stays inside with Mom. Across the fence, our neighbor's dog is lying on the cold concrete. She is chewing on something, and it must be sharp, because she spits it out with the same face she makes when she catches bees in the summer. I say her name *Molly* and open the door to the neighbor's yard. She seems scared of me for a second, and I understand why. I was angry last week when she went after the mail carrier. A swift leg to the chest. I hope she's forgiven me.

I walk slowly and see that she spit out a slightly crushed pest beetle. I pull it away, leave the yard, and place the beetle by our garage. It probably came from the neighbor's basement. I call the dog's name again when she sniffs back at an egress window, and she snaps out of the cycle for a moment, warm lab eyes at me, before she looks back again for another beetle.

I understand her. I also keep going back to what I shouldn't—the woods just beside the river.

FIVE THIRTY

Our dad's truck arrives home at five thirty, just fifteen minutes after we get back from school. Even though this is the way we've organized it for years, Max sucks in his breath every time.

Every time.

EMPIRE BUILDER

We once took a family trip on a train to Glacier National Park, Montana. Tucked in the *Empire Builder*, a two-story train, Max and I shared a blanket we still have. While Max sketched a ranch scene of Montana, I was content watching from the window as each span of land went by. I could tell by the hundreds of miles of brown grass in other states that Minnesota had an abundance of water.

I'm sure there's a reason God lets some land dry, other land grow, but when we returned home and saw the lakes and green grass, I knew I was blessed to live in a land that felt so alive. If Minnesota can somehow survive six months of winter and cold, maybe we can, too. Just a few more months before I can see green again.

AT SCHOOL

I finally see Nicole in the library checking out and returning books, her round glasses on the tip of her nose. I wonder if she'll be upset with me. My hands shake at the thought. I put them under the straps of my backpack and try to hold steady while I browse. I like reading anthropology, myths, anything ancient, especially math discoveries. I decide to keep my eyes to the shelves, but in a moment, Nicole is next to me, putting her books on the floor beside her black boots. She doesn't even question giving me a hug.

"Hey, I need your number," she says, and her tone is sure. Her short black hair a straight cut right at her chin.

"I was messaging you on Instagram and Snap."

She pulls away from the hug. "I deleted all my apps after moving. I miss my friends too much. I'm tired of seeing their stories and feeling jealous all the time." Her honesty reminds me of when we were little; it was hard to be fake with her. She hands me her phone after typing in the password. I smile, remembering we didn't have phones last time we went to school together.

"We're all old." She laughs like she read my mind.

"Yeah." I smile as I put my number in.

"You doing okay?" I ask, and hand her phone back. The last time I saw her—the police were talking to her separately, and she was ice-cold. Hardly answering them.

"Shitty. But, you know, I'm here," she says.

I want to say I'm sorry. That I hope she isn't mad at me. That I shouldn't have gone so far.

"Your hand is shaking," she says, looking down. Her dark eyebrows together and lips pursed.

I step away and shrug. "Happens sometimes."

She lifts an eyebrow. "They have you in counseling, right?"

"It sucks."

She laughs. "They're going to break you open like that kid in *Good Will Hunting*."

"Are they making you go, too?" I ask.

"To counseling? Nah, I've already got a therapist," she says. "I'm all set."

She picks up her books again, and I can see some of the stack she has. *She Would Be King*. *The Modern Herbal Dispensatory*. *Practicing Social Work Ethics Around the World*. They are definitely not for classes.

"Checking out the entire library?" I turn my head to read the other titles.

"This one was on my list." She taps the herbal dispensatory title. "They ordered it for me on my first day."

"Of course they did," I say. The warning bell goes off.

"I better go," she says, shrugging.

"Same. I'm sure I'll see you soon."

She nods. I turn to head toward English and look back just for a second. Nicole's eyes, which shined bright for the moments we talked, have now lost some of their fire.

I want to ask her what really happened in the woods. Where she and Luca were at. I've had no updates over our suspension except from one member of my calc group telling me that he saw Nicole and Luca walking together the other day. She didn't seem to hate me for beating him up, but she didn't tell me anything more, either.

WELCOME BACK TO DEER CREEK, MINNESOTA

After Nicole's parents split up, her mom stayed here in Deer Creek and her dad moved to Minneapolis. When I saw on Instagram that Nicole was moving back to Deer Creek over winter break to live with her mom, I didn't know what to think. In a way, it felt like family was moving home. Dad cut all his family out, Nicole's mom included, when he lost his job at the car dealership when we were fourteen.

Nicole's social media had gone quiet for a while, so it makes sense she wasn't getting my messages. Before she moved back, I hadn't sent her one message, unless it was on her birthday. But I did keep up, in a way. Her stories were always full of photos of her with friends, a former, I assume, boyfriend who looked like he really liked her. In some of her Instagram posts, she's wearing a jingle dress at powwows. In others, she's holding her new baby sister from her dad and his new girlfriend. The baby is really cute. She has the lightest brown skin, pink lips, and dark hair. Another post was of her and Luca getting dinner in Minneapolis. Her last post was a photo of Nicole with her mom at the sale of a house in Deer Creek, announcing that she was moving and would finish her last year and a half of high school here. It was in November, and Shelly and Nicole both wore big warm jackets and beaded bright earrings that I'd seen in Tia's online shop.

I don't know why she'd leave the city for Deer Creek. This half-suburb, half–small town that gets its brightness only from the 7-Eleven signs and maple leaves in the fall. Maybe she misses her mom. Shelly is a socialite. Always on top of things. The busiest person. She's on signs all around town for her booming realty business.

I asked Max what he thought, showing him the photo of Nicole and her mom smiling in front of a sold sign.

He laughed. "Yeah. If I were her, I'd never move back here," he said dryly.

I still remember the first day of school after Nicole moved in with her dad in Minneapolis. Max and me, all of a sudden, the only Native kids here.

Her most recent post was during winter break, a photo of her and Luca in the snow at a tree farm. He's holding her from behind, kissing her cheek, and she's laughing.

And what had we done, right when Nicole got back? How could she hug me like that after what I did to Luca? But she did today.

INTERCOM

They read Max's and my name along with fifty others, all on the honor roll from last semester. Pins are being sold. Stickers are available.

At home, Max and I put the stickers on the kitchen table, and Dad puts one on each side of his bumper. We shake our heads as we watch him from the living room window.

"What an asshole," Max says, his arms crossed.

LUCA

For our first meeting with Luca, Max is leaning back in his chair, and I know he has little remorse. *We are not our father*, he told me in all surety when I couldn't sleep last night. *We didn't know what was happening. We did what we could for what we saw.* And every time, I want to believe him. But when I see Luca, the healing bruises on his nose, a soft purple on his light brown skin, over his brow beneath dark hair, I am unsure if I went too far. If I could have stopped.

In our meeting, Luca doesn't say anything. He looks expectant.

I'm sorry, I say, *that we hurt you.*

Max turns and eyes me.

I'm sorry, I rephrase, *that I hurt you.*

I want Max to say something, too, because we need to prove to our school that we are decent people. If we don't do these talks and counseling, it will make getting into college difficult. Not that I worry too much about myself, because I don't know if I could leave Mom.

Max wants to go big and get out. His target art school's opening deadline was earlier this month, but he decided to wait for its last application date to have a better chance at proving himself. So I'm doing this for him and, I don't know, a little for me. But Max is not about it. He wants his pride *and* art school. He is looking right into Luca's eyes while Luca sits in a chair across from us. Silent.

Our counselor says, *I think we are done for today. We'll come back together in two weeks.*

GRANDPA FERNANDO

Our grandpa on Mom's side is named Fernando Ortiz. He has a doctorate in art studies from the University of Minnesota. He likes jazz and speaks three languages. In other words, he can speak back through generations of colonization—through English, through Spanish conquest—to our people, among the first peoples of modern-day Costa Rica, the Bribri. Before my father closed our doors to family, Grandpa would come over, sit on the couch, and tell us stories about our people, our ancestors. He'd tell us of tricksters, the Creator Sibö, and men who were cursed after selfishness. He'd explain why we wore long hair to keep us safe while walking in the rain forest, when we could be attacked from above. How our hair is an extension of ourselves. He'd tell us about his mother giving birth to him alone by the river. He taught us to call our traditional land Talamanca. The land of mountains and jungle. Grandpa Fernando reminded us that we are the people grown out of the earth itself. And how Bribri means just that—people of the uneven land.

Grandpa Fernando used to bring us pictures of his parents, his siblings, now all passed. They look like us—wide-cheeked, wide-nosed, smooth brown skin. In his favorite photo, our great-aunts and great-uncles wore thick rubber boots, thin cotton clothing, and our great-grandma wore her hair in two braids. Our people have a strength of continuance despite Spanish efforts. We continue to dance our dances. Our language is spoken, and our stories are still alive, even if I don't know them all yet. We have greetings like 'Ìs be' shkèna, Bua'ë Bua'ë and mountains like Kamu to hold us steady in the midst of sorrow.

I shame at my warrior tendencies. Our people are not known for using our fists; we are still here because we know who we are and lean on the stories to remind us. Have I shifted the balance? I already know Grandpa would shake his head at me if he knew what I did in the woods. Mom and the rest of us are good at keeping secrets, at hiding mistakes, but this does not feel very Bribri of us, either.

LANGUAGE LESSONS

When Grandpa used to stay over, I would hear him speaking and singing Bribri in the shower. The whisper over the running water could calm me any day. He taught us words we say now when we call him.

Dawö'chke, he calls us.

Dawö'chke, we call him.

The name is relationship, one grandfather to grandson and back again. The word sounds like the coo of a bird. I have always wanted to become Grandpa Fernando and would never call Dad anything in Bribri. At least not now. When I was little, I'd call him yë'. I silently hope, when Grandpa calls me dawö'chke, that maybe he can see himself in me.

A STORY OF OUR NAMES

Our people's stories can take months to tell. And our tradition is, you can only share one or two in a day. Nearly everything has a story. The woodpeckers, the foxes, the butterflies. This story of Sibö the Creator's birth is from before fertile earth existed and during a time when the underworlds were made entirely of spirit. A spirit in a bad spiritual layer named Sibökma, three layers down from earth, wondered if goodness existed elsewhere. You see, Sibökma was imaginative—he foresaw a new plane, one made of stars, one for the moon, another for lush green land and even animals. He left his evil plane in the underworld to find a place to create. And along the way met a good spirit of another layer, and they jumped past the spiritual worlds to a bare physical plane. Soon his good spirit companion became pregnant, and they had to return to Sibökma's home so she could give birth. But the evil spirits sought to attack her as she carried a child of two planes, two worlds.

When she finally gave birth to Sibö the Creator, a rooster crowed to the king of evil spirits, and Sibö's mother had to flee with her infant. She escaped to another good spiritual plane. There, Sibö grew and strengthened, and he took his mother's name before he began to create the world his father imagined.

This is why our people carry our mother's last names and why each clan is maternal. This is why Grandpa Fernando took Grandma's last name when they married and moved from Costa Rica to the United States. And why Max and I took Mom's last name, Ortiz. Why we are Mudiwak from our mother, the Ash Creek Fish Clan. I consider our name a gift. It is a gift to be reminded of our capability of good. For thousands of years our people steadied our children into a light direction despite evil equally residing in us. I remember this with each dark gleam in our father's eye and each light gleam in our mother's.

The women are the better of us, and our people know this.

IN THE WOODS

Max and I would often go to the Mississippi River when we knew Dad was at work. Before the river, there are woods. On winter break, we were walking through the trees when we heard shouts in a voice like and unlike our mother's. I looked at Max. He looked at me. We ran in through spruce and leafless maple, our boots smashing into snowy ground, hearing deep-voiced threats all the way to a clearing. That's where we found Nicole and Luca.

Luca was pulling at her jacket, and she pushed his hands away. Then Luca's hands were on her shoulders while she swore at him. He had a hand out as if to explain. She pushed him off, then he grabbed her hand and yanked it down and then leaned forward to say something in her ear.

And we snapped.

We were on him, pulling him away from Nicole, and he swore at us. He shoved Max, and I shoved him back, then he shoved me back, and then we beat the heck out of him.

No, we beat the *hell* out of him.

And we could hardly stop.

We would take a break and say we should stop, but then one of us would start again, but then the other would join in until Nicole said both our names. "Max. Jay." She woke us up, her head in her hands.

We called for an ambulance. We all waited silently on a log while bloody-faced Luca lay on the ground moaning.

We had just beat up the captain of the soccer team. The sweetheart of Deer Creek.

POWER OF TWO

Mom has always said that the strength of two was something special. A rope binding together. She meant Max or me marrying someday. I think she still thinks of her and Dad that way. Two people who connected over the early deaths of their mothers. He was kinder then. Respectful of our traditions. Letting us have her name. Being a father who'd show up to our soccer games, who loved Mom's hot chocolate. I think he did love her before he forgot how. And I think of how Nicole deserves someone who doesn't treat her like Luca did. How she deserves so much more.

Max and I are another kind of rope tie. There is an Old Testament story where a man named Jonathan risks his life for King David, and a verse says that David loved Jonathan with more love than a man had for a woman—and Max and I are like that. Brothers born eleven months apart. Now in the same senior class of high school. No one sneaks up on us. When I shake, Max speaks for me. When Max cries at night, I close his bedroom door for him. We give more for each other than our father does for our mother.

We move like one.

FIRSTS

Almost four years ago, on Max's fourteenth birthday, Dad lost his job at the Ford plant. A small recession had hit Minnesota. No one was buying new cars.

Mom made a cake for Max, and Dad cried. He seemed frustrated at the small expense of our family take-out dinner. Later that night, I listened through the bedroom door while Dad called his father, Grandpa Greer, and asked if he could borrow some money for the week. The plant had cut off pay that day. On the other line, I heard swearing and a loud voice telling Dad that he needed to pull himself together, that he needed to be a man and provide for his own damn family.

Then there was only a beep for a hang up. Dad opened the door and caught me listening. I saw his usual hard anger turned hot, but hotter this time. I can still feel it.

That first time he swung.

My body crumpled onto the wooden floor.

He knew I wouldn't tell Max. Not on his birthday. I remember lying there while my body shook. I could hear Max's favorite movie on downstairs and screeching—the throwback *TRON*—and Mom's hands bustling with the dishes.

I knew I needed to get up, my head ringing.

But I didn't know this would become my new life.

SECRETS

Despite hurting Luca pretty bad, no one was pressing charges, but school found out about it. We explained that we thought he was going to hurt her, but it wasn't enough to get us out of a counseling plan. Luca had only pulled Nicole's arm down, even if we both felt like he was going to do more. We reacted.

After our meeting, I ask myself what the counselor did the first day. *Why couldn't you have just stopped? Why couldn't you have just stepped in. Why didn't I stop? Why did I have to go so far?*

"Take your hands off me," Nicole said in the woods.

He was shouting at her. "What the hell, Nicole?"

And then her again. "Get off me."

His hand grabbing hers, pulling her toward him, some inaudible whisper. His eyes too familiar.

All I can do is show up to counseling sessions. The pangs of remorse feel more like flipping over and showing my stomach.

What we know is anger, and I know what men are capable of.

This is why we went *that far*.

7-ELEVEN GAS STATION

Ice water and more ice water. At the gas station, so many people come in and ask me for free water. Minnesota license plates or not. Costing the gas station—the cup, the time, the ice—thirty-five cents. I notice my chest lighten every time I nod and say it's fine to take a free cup at the dispenser. Max and I used to ask for water all the time while we waited for Dad to pick us up here on Saturday afternoons. It is the one free thing you can get at the 7-Eleven. Because who is going to deny you water? So here at work, the folks who come in don't know who I am, ask for a drink, and for a moment I get to be the kind person and say, "Yes."

For hours I stand behind the counter at the cash register. From here I can see where Max and I used to wait on the bench outside for Dad. It's empty.

Every season, something as simple as this bench gains a new layer of memory. One layer of memory, Max and I leaning back, sweaty, while we take turns drinking from an extra-large cup of water. A second layer, when Nicole's mom was actually on the advertisement, her photo on the back of the bench for her real estate business. The third layer is a seasonal memory, when the winter snow stacks up like seat cushions. A distant fourth layer, Dad sitting there with us, his arms stretched, an arm behind each of us. Tugging playfully on my baseball cap. Our meeting spot after playing in the park.

I rub my forehead. I take a moment to stare again at today's layer—empty and slightly damp from the light snow. I bite my lips because my chest is heavy again and pray, *God, why is this so hard?* I turn and look around the station to confirm, yes. No one is here.

I sit on the floor and pull out my phone to message Nicole.

JAY: You ready to move back to Minneapolis yet?

NICOLE: Ha. It's not so bad. I honestly like getting to see more lakes and water again here. All the trees and stuff.

JAY: People been nice to you?

NICOLE: A few girls who were friends in middle school have reached out.

JAY: That's cool. Do you like them?

NICOLE: I mean they're nice. But I miss my Minneapolis friends.

JAY: Yeah that makes sense. We should sit by each other for lunch sometime.

NICOLE: Sure.

JAY: Can I ask you a question and you don't have to answer it?

NICOLE: Can I stop you?

JAY: Ha sorry. I'm just wondering if you and Luca are still together? Or?

NICOLE: Oh yeah. We're working on things. I don't really want to talk about it though.

JAY: Totally get it. I guess I'm just feeling guilty that I didn't catch up with you after you moved. And then the first time we see each other I'm like beating the shit out of your bf. So I'm sorry.

NICOLE: Yeah I know. But we're family.

JAY: Thanks, Nicole.

JAY: So how is Tia? What is she up to?

NICOLE: Overachieving. Studying art in Santa Fe. She's like really good at beading and got her own website where she sells her stuff and is making bank. Mom is *beaming* and wears her stuff every time she has a showing.

JAY: Sounds like Tia.

NICOLE: Yeah. She's a lot. Ha. Oh shoot. I have to go.

JAY: Okay. Bye.

NICOLE: Bye.

I keep thinking about some of her spirit looking so tired at school. Nicole is the most capable person I know. Her wanting to work things through with Luca is being mature. He has always been a really nice guy at school. I know he coaches kids in need over the summers. And that photo of him kissing her . . . maybe he's allowed to get upset just once. And then I wonder if I should just leave Nicole alone now.

The bell on the door rings, and I flinch because I know my shift is almost done. It's Gabe. The next shift. He peers over the counter. "You good, man?"

"Yeah." I stand and brush the floor's dirt off my pants. "Had nothing better to do."

"I feel that," he says.

THE SWEETHEART OF DEER CREEK

His soccer moves are like magic. Luca brings out the *pretty moves*. The Latin American moves we know only come from hours and hours of playing pickup and watching games with his family. The twirls, the rainbows, the arcs right into the corner pockets of the net, a shot made from all the way out of the box. A forward like our school has never seen.

He's been the best since we were in elementary school. We knew his dad from our 10U recreational team. He's a professor at the college. I remember him being really intense at our practices, yelling at Luca on the sidelines, pushing him to do better. In a way, his family looked somewhat like ours—his mom from Mexico, dad from here. We even went over to his house a couple of times for birthday parties. Luca actually spoke some Spanish to us like we were insiders, which isn't all that common here in Deer Creek. Even if the Spanish were our colonizers, and we don't even speak that much of it, it was kind of a nice thing.

When I think about him lying on the ground, I guess I am sorry. A soccer player doesn't ever have to learn to fight. Max and I shouldn't know how to take down a full-grown man. Luca is another kind of brother maybe.

INDIGENOUS RESISTANCE

The whispers are everywhere, and I get a few more hard looks at school. I check Snap and see that Luca shared a story last night that he's healing up fine, happy to be back at school, that Nicole didn't do anything wrong, and that he cares so about her and is so grateful they are together. He is driving his dad's Jeep and talking, smiling and slightly distracted.

He doesn't say anything about us. He doesn't say how he'd been suspended and given community service, too. He doesn't say anything about doing wrong, and that's what makes me a little upset. It seems that everyone at school is following along with him. He's smoothing this all over as if what he did never happened. We might be the only people who have ever seen that side of him. Well, us and Nicole.

It's lunchtime, and I find Nicole with her arms full of books, trying to open her locker. She's wearing her sister's designer jean jacket that has an American flag upside down. *Indigenous* is stitched above the flag, and *resistance* below. *Defoe* is her last name on a patch on the shoulder. A few friends are around her, and she opens her locker, puts her books in, and then hugs a couple of them. They look at her, all smiles.

I hear one girl say how cool Nicole's jacket is, and then another goes to stroke her hair that is pulled back on one side with a pin—and Nicole puts her hand up and shakes her head. *Stop.*

The girl pulls her hand back sheepishly. "Sorry, that's so rude. You're right," the girl says. I almost laugh as I walk by. I know how often our hair gets touched by some older white woman on the bus, the street, a school event.

"Jay," I hear. I glance back, and Nicole shoots me a look like *I'm getting the hell out of here*. I laugh while the girls look at me like I'm going to eat them. "Lunch?"

"I like your hair," I tease.

"Shut up." We laugh together because I think we both know sometimes all you can do is laugh through this shit. But I don't know if either of us is ready to laugh it all off.

HALLWAY

Nicole walks with me to get my lunch, and we turn into the hallway toward my locker. More people arc just slightly away from me. Even Derek from calculus. He keeps his head down.

I spot Luca. He's got his arm around one of his teammates and a freshman girl; I'm forgetting her name. Soccer player, I think. They're watching a video on someone's phone. One of his teammates goes, "See, look at that move! Right there. And the shot! Perfection." The freshman leans in closer to Luca.

I turn and see Nicole bite her lips.

One of his teammates sees me coming and thins his eyes at me. Luca looks up just a second later, his eyes widening for half a second, but then casually takes his arm off his friend, then the freshman, and waves at Nicole.

"Hey, Nicole! Saw your mom sold our neighbor's huge house on the lake!"

"Yeah, it's a winner," Nicole says half-heartedly.

I wish it was hard to believe Nicole would like him, but lots and lots of girls have had crushes on Luca since middle school. Not just the soccer group; he is one of those people who makes friends everywhere. Bright smile. A friendly husk in his voice. The freshman was clearly swooning under his cozy friendship. I do remember Nicole waving at him whenever he got on the bus to middle school. *Hey, Luca. Hey, Luca. Hey, Luca.* I guess I remember wanting to be his friend when we were younger.

I look back at Nicole, and she tosses her head in the opposite direction.

"I think I'm going to go home," she says in a low voice. "Can you ask Ms. Constant to send the test to the library for me?"

I nod because I know better than to push. Damn, Nicole can do anything she wants. Maybe it's that Nicole is family, but I can't help but want to take Luca out all over again. I can't make up my freaking mind.

APOLOGIES

Dad never apologizes. After Max's fourteenth birthday, he took to hitting me whenever I did anything that upset him. He is good at finding hidden spaces to inflict some form of pain, especially when he drinks.

Then he started on Max.

He made us swear never to tell Mom, because she wouldn't understand that it was what we deserved for acting like fools, for not doing what he asked, for looking at him the wrong way and how it showed him disrespect. That didn't last long, because his anger turned to her soon. At night, Max would tell me what happened if I had been gone. He'd whisper it so quietly that Dad had no chance of hearing. *When I'm older, he's going to be sorry*, I'd tell Max. *I'll show him how it feels.*

CHURCH BROWN

Max sells one of his dark paintings to our pastor, and it now hangs up in the church lobby. The walls are already muted brown, so a dark canvas doesn't do much. A little plaque with his name on it is knocked into the wall. UNTITLED NO. 19. MAX ORTIZ.

"It's abstract," Max says. "I've been working on that."

When I stare into it, it's as if I'm staring death in the eye, through thick layers and buried colors. That feeling of darkness is so familiar I have to look away. How can he even create right now?

I swallow. "It's good."

SUNDAY EVENING

Dad rides to a friend's house to watch the Super Bowl after church, and Mom stays behind for a baby shower, and I figure we have a little time. I take Dad's truck keys from the basket above the stove and toss them to Max. He smiles at me. We are thinking, *why the hell not?*

Max drives, and I open one of the Cokes I snagged from Dad's fridge downstairs, where he keeps all his lemons, limes, Cokes, and Sprites. He likes rum and Coke. We'll pick up whatever I use from the gas station afterward. I text Nicole if she wants to come, but she says she can't.

I roll down the window all the way, stick my feet up on the side-view mirror since that's the only way I'll fit. There's a shock of cold air when Max hits the gas, but it's not bad for the first week of February. In the corner of my eye, I see Max grinning just a little. It's that moment where brotherhood just is—you're not trying, but you can't help but feel it. If I could, I'd spend the rest of my days next to Max with no particular place to go. I know him so well that I do already know where we are going first: the field.

It comes up and over a hill about four miles out of town—a dead grass field. Come April, it will stud with green blades. And by late spring, the spread of budding goldenrod will come, and the whole field ignites gold. We used to sit out there for hours. Max, drawing. Me, writing whatever I noticed that day.

"I wish I could get it down on a canvas," Max says. "I keep trying from memory, but I'm not good enough yet."

"Must be hard to not be good enough yet." I laugh and take a swig.

"You know that's not what I mean," he says.

"It's just a bunch of weeds in their prime." I bump his shoulder with my Coke bottle to make him look at the land again before I take another sip.

"Don't act like you don't have anything you're good at. You'll ace a math test without even studying. And then, what, you got a freaking five on your last AP History test?"

I shake my head at him. He likes to do that to me all the time when I make fun of him. Give me a compliment. The upper hand.

I open the glove box and find a magazine Dad stashed there. A woman with a low-cut shirt leans forward on the cover. My face warms for a second, and then I bite my cheek because it's ridiculous our father would pine for someone else when he harms Mom under our roof.

"Nice," I say, and show it to Max.

"He really needs help."

"You're preaching to a choir here."

I shove the magazine back into the glove box.

"Hey, so how is Nicole doing?" Max asks.

"I don't know. I feel like she still really likes Luca. But she kinda seems down. Not the normal Nicole, you know?"

"I swear we're all depressed. Some generational trauma or something," Max says. "But honestly, after he pulled that shit in the woods, he doesn't deserve her. I don't care what anyone says." Max's sureness is what I need. The way he sees the world, the real colors of people.

"So you're really, really trying for art school?" I ask.

"Yup." He drums on the wheel. "I've got two months to prep. Thank goodness for MCAD's deadlines. They are pretty lax."

"Yeah. All you artists, you can't keep a schedule and they know that," I tease him despite my heart dropping at the thought of his wanting to leave. I look out the window and stay quiet.

I know he wants his school record to look right. Our transcripts include grades, attendance, behavior. The first semester of senior year and our early winter break suspension fall under that. Applying late is the best chance for him to own his suspension and show the ways he's working toward change.

We decide to drive Dad's truck out as far as an hour will take us, and it does feel good to get away. Maybe a little holy with the windows down even when it's cold, free as anything. But I don't know how long we'll get to have this.

THE TWO MEN AND THE MYSTICAL EAGLES

Growing up, Mom would tell us the story of the mystical eagles so often before bed that I can't remember *not* knowing it. The mystical eagles were the dragons of Talamanca. Large beaks, black inky wings, and machete talons. They'd come down from the mountains, tearing children from their mothers' arms, snatching those who went out in the day from the pathways. The mystical eagles had become so terrifying that our people didn't leave home in fear of never returning.

The whole tribe decided to fast, and two young men were chosen to stop the eagles. They went to their Awa, and he blessed their knives, rope, and tobacco. Then a few women wove a basket so large, so strong, with huge handles so it would be easy to snatch and carry. In the night, the men slipped into the basket and the female eagle came and took it high to a nest of bones where her two growing chicks were hungry. There, the two young men smoked the tobacco and, like bees, the female and two young mystical chicks fell asleep, then fell from the mountain to their deaths. Finally, the male eagle came, and the men again began to smoke, and he, too, fell asleep. And while he did, they swiftly took a knife to his throat and cut him to pieces.

They had succeeded.

Then the men looked down from the nest and could see their people's homes. With their rope, they lowered themselves from the mountain right down to Sibödi or the River Where Sibö Swam. There, they made a canoe that led them back to Talamanca, where our people were finally safe.

The mystical eagles never returned.

LATE

We are too late. Dad comes home early on Monday after school, and we walk into yelling. Yelling and worse.

Mom is on the couch crying, holding her shoulder. Her braid is pulled to one side. Max goes to her, and when I look at Dad, his hand clenched, I think of what Max said, how no one deserves this. I don't hesitate. With two long strides, I am right up to him, him and his sour breath. I send my fist right to his face. He wavers for a moment, steadies himself with his back to the living room wall. When he is about to lunge at me, I grab his shoulder and Max grabs his arms.

"Do you see what you did to her? Do you?" I yell at Dad and point to Mom. His mouth opens like he's about to harden or soften, but before he says anything, he rips his arms out of Max's grip, takes the keys, and leaves the house.

WORKOUT

I wake up early and check on Mom. Only her breathing is raising the quilt. I glance down the stairs, and Max is still sleeping on the couch by the door as a lookout. It's clear for me to go on a run. The thrill of Dad's leaving for a night gets me pumped. My sweats and sweatshirt are laid out on my bed, and before I put them on, I can't help but smile in the mirror. All the push-ups I do at work and before bed are showing up, and I see the height I've grown this year. Maybe this is what I really want. Maybe it finally made Dad regret hitting us in the first place. We don't need his construction money, and we could all move. Mom, Max, and me. When I pull on my sweatpants, the elastic stops a few inches above my ankles. I pull on tall black socks so it looks like it's on purpose.

I look like I'm getting ready to mess with someone, but really, I've just got this light smile on my lips. Like maybe a few people would cross the street when they see me running. But I'm not crossing the street for their comfort. Not today. I quietly walk by Max, lock the door with my house key, and I'm outside in the cool morning air. I jog to the nearby park, my breath a fog. There, I do leg stretches, and my muscles liberate. I do pull-ups on the cold metal monkey bars. This is what tells me I am not a child anymore. My arms bulk as I pull, and the strength feels good. I never feel stronger than when I'm working out.

The whole world could be messing with me, but I'll still have an edge.

FISTS

Nicole comes to the lunchroom with me, and her eyes linger on my bruised hand when I reach for a fruit punch at the checkout. I almost laugh at how ironic it is. Fruit punch.

"Where did that come from?" she asks as we pay the lunch person.

I flash her the back of my hand. "Wall," I say.

Nicole nods like she only half believes me. "Poor wall."

I follow her toward the hallway on the third floor where no one ever is. Maybe to avoid any more run-ins with Luca.

"Are you doing okay?" I ask.

"I don't know."

"It wasn't exactly super cool that Luca was hanging with that freshman."

"Yeah. I know."

I am a little braver after last night. "You know we had to talk to Luca last week." I sit down on the floor, back to a locker.

"Mhmmm." She sits next to me.

"He didn't say anything, just stared at us." I open my cheese stick.

"Okay."

"What do you think about that?" I side-eye her.

"I don't know, Jay." She unwraps her veggie sandwich and takes a bite. Swallows. Then she sighs and leans back on the locker next to me. "I don't think that everyone can be defined by one bad decision," she says. "The whole thing you guys showed up to was that. Afterward he said he was sorry and would never do it again, and I trust him. And he was just introducing that girl to his friends since he thought she has a good shot at varsity next year. So he wasn't trying to get away with anything." She doesn't look me in the eyes. I wonder if she really believes this.

"It didn't look like that to me."

"Well, I've screwed up relationships before. I've been the irrational, unforgiving one in a relationship. And I ruined it with my last boyfriend. I don't want to do that here."

"I can't imagine you being irrational."

"I'm human, Jay. You're human. I'm still hanging out with you. And no one else is."

Her words sting. She's not wrong.

I remember the way that Luca looked at her in the woods. It reminded me of my dad, how he looked last night. I pray to God I don't have that look. That look that says, *I'm the world, I do no wrong.*

And Luca seems to want everyone to know he's done no wrong.

COUNSELING

I pull down my long sleeve over my hand before we sit in the fabric chairs. The high of Dad's departure is wearing off, especially after my talk with Nicole. I never hit Dad so hard that he left before. I'd let him have it, and he'd hit me back and then storm off downstairs. Never went for the keys and left. I try to shake it off.

"How's it going, Picasso?" I ask Max while we wait.

He smiles. "Fine."

Ms. Hannan walks in, a clipboard in her hand. I wonder what her files say about us.

"Let's talk about home," she says warmly while she flips on her water heater.

Max and I don't even look at each other. "Nothing to talk about," Max says coolly.

"How is your mother? What does she do for work?"

"She doesn't work," I say.

"And Dad?"

"Why does it matter? What does that have to do with Luca?" Max says. He looks at me and shakes his head while she writes something down on her notepad.

"I want you each to spend some time here journaling about your parents, your family. A not-so-good time and a good time."

I think of what Nicole said about people not being defined by one bad decision. And my chest gets heavy with a memory of when I was eight. Dad made us pancakes and took us rollerblading around the neighborhood. He let Mom sleep in. We were so excited to wake up and smell syrup and butter. Scrambling over each other down the stairs, trying to remember to keep our voices low.

We're never going to ever be there again. In those kinds of memories, Dad had never done what he has now. He's never done wrong over and over again. God, do I wish whatever that was could have stayed.

I just write down *pancakes*.

SHIFTS

When I started working at 7-Eleven last year, we created shifts. When I was at the gas station, Max would stay home with Mom to be there when Dad came home. And, in turn, when I wasn't working, I was at home with Mom and Max would get a night to be alone, draw, paint, or whatever he's working on now.

I hate it, but Dad comes home this afternoon. I stayed with Mom just in case, hoping Dad would stay gone for a second night. He doesn't look at me when he comes in. He goes to the basement. I can hear the TV turn on. I already know that if I'm here, he's not trying anything.

Usually Max just spends his evenings "off" sketching in his room. Nicole is right in a lot of ways—we don't really have friends or anyone to hang with.

But tonight, Max asks Mom for her keys.

I almost ask him where he's going, but it's not like he asks me where I go when I'm leaving for work or go on a run.

II
MAX

…

Mom's cries last night
stick with me—
they flash a bright,
painful green.

I fell asleep crying,
woke up, sore and
salty on my face.

My hands are overstretched
from holding Dad's
arms back last night.

For once, I want to see
the beauty of the world

flung back
at me.

…

...

From the garage,
I get my painting
stuff, place my school easel
in the passenger seat,
paints in a bag,
and with Mom's keys,
my hand to the wheel,
foot to pedal, I leave.
Leaving is a breath of clean,
just-rained air,
even if it really
is the dullest February.

...

…

I expect a tree to speak to me
or a broken light
in a parking lot.
But near the river,
when I drive past the trailer park,
I see Melody.

…

…

There's a vivid backdrop.
Dark dead grass of the flat park.

Melody, a person I've known since
elementary school. We all know one another
here. She sits at a red swing
in a dress and boots.

Hair autumnal, natural, but loud
red, and her skin—red-blotchy and light.
Her hands on the lower chain
links of the swing, while she looks
the opposite way down the road.

I've asked people if I could paint them
before. Sometimes yes, and sometimes no.

…

…
Because in my mind,
everyone is
a painting,
waiting.

I can ask the trees for permission
and they know me so well,
they don't often say no.

But now,
I'm biting my cheeks,
looking down at my bag,
paints adding up.
…

...

I flinch when I look
through the back of the car again.

My body turns with a slower
pace of the same move Dad
would make to give us,
          in the back seat, a slap,

but something pulls me
                    to still reach for Jay's sweater
                    he's left there. I put it on.

...

...

I get out of the car,
take my easel, canvas, bag, and
walk toward the playground.

Jay's voice whispering *don't,*
another says she might
see me as *no good.*

I see Nicole, more family, her arms thrown down.
I hear me telling me that I cannot trust myself.

A counselor telling me to
Share, Max. Share.

But then a muddy breeze hits
me and lifts bumps on my arms.

I welcome them and I answer
these voices
with *no.*

...

…
In a minute,
I'm in front of Melody's swing.

She's looking at me and my easel
like she is working out why
I'm coming over. At school,
sometimes she's looked sad for me.
There are a few people like that—
they don't talk to us, but they look
like they could.

Hey, Max, she says. I don't know
the last time anyone said hi to me.
No one from school anyway, and
never Dad.

Hi, Melody. I was driving by
and I wondered if I could paint you?

Her eyebrows are really chill,
even, and she says, *Sure, Max.*
…

…

I set up my easel,
lean a canvas to my leg, a cheap one
from a set Jay bought for me
over Christmas. I already
know he'd wonder why
I'd make time to paint a girl
I hardly know. *Everyone hates us.*

I move, piece by piece,
tightening the legs,
propping the back to the
best angle, setting
up in the damp sandpit.

I see Melody's brown eyes looking
at my fingers and
my paints.

…

...
I breathe.
When you look at a subject,
the face they give you isn't
always the one you're going
to paint. Plenty
of people pose
as who they want to be,
and you have to pose
them back on the canvas.

But Melody
stays just so. Still in her
former attitude.

Maybe this is what makes me
know why I had
to pull over.
...

…
You can feel free to talk if you want,
I say.

Cool,
she says.

We're quiet for a while. I get
a background color in my
gray acrylic paint.

So how is your semester going?
I ask.

It's going well. You know, I like photography.
So I see maybe why you'd pick this spot.
She smiles.
Ever put yourself in a scene just because
it feels right? she asks.

All the time, I say.
I even think about the couch
this morning. And any time with the trees.
…

…
I've seen your paintings in the studio. They're good.
I like the large one with all the black.

Thanks, I say.

Are you going to paint like that for this one?

Nah. I think there's a lot going on here. I smile.
…

…

I finish the background. It's a pale
gray haze out today. <u>Gray</u>.

Tell me about photography. I look at my palette.

I mean, I like it. But I don't know if it's the thing,
you know?

Sure, I say, even though I don't. Already lying.
I've always known what I've wanted to do since I had paper,
colors. I couldn't be surer about it.

…

…

A rightful distraction. <u>Red.</u>
Can I ask you a question? she says.

Sure.

I mean, I'm not a person for drama, but
are you okay after all that happening over break with
your cousin and brother and everything?

I'm fine.

I am just wondering because
I do feel like there is always more
than one side, you know?

You saying you're on mine? I shake my head
and laugh.

Well, you don't seem like a coldhearted jackass.

I smile, but I don't know if I believe her words.

…

…

We thought Luca was going to hurt Nicole.
I mean, I guess we didn't know for sure if he
would. But I feel like I knew.
They were upset at each other in the woods.

I don't know why I am saying anything.

I've written everyone off because I've
got just under four and a half months of school to
get through.
And one art school application to land.

See, that doesn't seem like a jerk to me.

I shrug. I pick <u>Brown.</u> <u>Silver.</u>
…

…

We're quiet for a while.
The swing and the trailer home structures
are in, and I start her facial outline,
lineation I've been practicing.

So tell me about painting. She asks
me my own question.
I am not really sure how to *tell* about art.
If I wasn't trying to keep my cool, I'd tell her everything.
I would say that I'd die for art.
I'd tell her how much I love
the trees, how color is like
music.

How much I hunger
for that feeling of dreaming
when I walk into the studio.

That if I were to have her hum
low, that is how deep it is
for me to create. Like
I'm agreeing with God.

…

…

From wound to art, I say, repeating what
our art teacher says all the time.
*It's basic, but sometimes the basics
are true*, I add.
She nods in agreement.

But then I get that feeling I do,
to *make art* is selfish.

To art is forgetful, even
if what I try to forget still finds
its way on the canvas; even in
its absence, I am avoiding it all,
wanting everything else I've
never had.

…

…
We talk on, and
Melody is made of color.

She tells me she doesn't
know what she wants to be, although she likes
photography, which is how she saw my work.
She says she envies people like me
who just seem to *know*.

I haven't thought of someone being
jealous of me.

But when she says this,
she seems to be more honest
than most people I know. Really
sure of herself.

She asks,
*Is it okay that I
moved a little?*

Yeah, all good.
…

…
I try to pay attention to the
surrounding trailer park.

There, a smoking empty bean can
with cigarette butts on the steps
of one trailer home.

A kiddie park
pool with a centimeter of
winter water, a pink bottle of
bubbles floats, then the matted cats,
and distant unoccupied lawn chairs,

until it finally gets really cold,
and everything
is glowing.
…

...
I lend her the sweater I'm wearing,
even if it's Jay's,
because what else can I do?
...

. . .

Her parents, a mother/photographer, too, a
father, steady as the Mississippi
to the Gulf, a hopeful playwright.
Her parents agreed no one would give up
their art when Melody was born.

And then I'm done.
And it's good. I can tell.
I used paints I hadn't used
yet. Block colors, clean lines,
then Melody.

I look at it for a bit, the painting
for the last moment, just for me
to see.

. . .

...

I show her, and she
smiles while her eyes
seem to outline each
structure, and soften
on herself.

I hope she doesn't
mind that I've painted
her slight shrug, but to me
she is a full self.
Really nice, she says.
I breathe small relief.

...

...

Can I give you my number? Melody asks.
I pull out my phone, unlock it,
and hand it to her.

...

…
If she's let me dream
for an hour, what can I do but
want to more?
…

III
JAY

MOM

I see a bruise on Mom's forearm when I get home from work on Thursday. It looks new, despite Dad supposedly staying at his co-worker's last night because his hours were running late. Despite us taking our shifts, standing guard. I can see she tried to cover it up with chalky makeup. I can always tell.

It had been my work shift, so it was Max's turn to be with Mom.

"Dad come home?" I ask.

She looks away from me and pulls her fingers through her hair.

"Wasn't Max here?" I ask.

"He doesn't need to be here every day, Jay."

Dammit, Max. Where the hell were you?

TEN P.M.

I would have talked to Max about leaving Mom, but we get a call from the police department before Max even gets home from who knows where.

Dad is sitting in the precinct for unpaid parking tickets. I remember him sitting in our living room for the whole recession year. Max and I in eighth grade learning to not upset him while he watched TV. He'd sit there, drink, and get angrier. Mom picking up side jobs so he didn't have to worry. It was Mom who found him a job in construction, something he used to do as a teenager. It was one of their worst fights, but he got himself ready the next day for the interview, a flask in his old work boots.

He never admits that Mom found him the job. After he got it, he'd gloat to people at church about providing for our family. That the recession was hard, but he was doing his duty, pulling himself back up. But he never dropped the drinking. Never stopped the anger. The power he'd grown to enjoy over us. He quickly had Mom quit all her jobs, kept her at home.

Apparently, he and his coworker were out earlier this evening, and he was pulled over for tickets he hadn't paid for the last year. He has been working construction in downtown Bemidji. He tells Mom that he meant to pay them, that this was *ridiculous*.

We all know the fine is too big, and so two days in jail it is.

It is two more days that he'll be away from us.

DAY ONE

With Dad gone, I decide to take my time after school. I don't want to go home for a while. I ask if I could go to Nicole's house after, but she says it'd be better if we went to Turtle Lake, because her mom has a client party. I invite Max, but he texts me he's going to stay and paint, probably just to avoid me since I know he saw Mom's bruise when he got home late last night, easel in one arm. She told him right away that Dad was staying at the precinct. He knows I'm upset with him, because he wouldn't look me in the eyes.

Turtle Lake is the opposite way of the Mississippi River and on a land reserve. Small trails and tall woods, until a boardwalk through marsh. I want to tell Nicole that my dad is in jail. I want to tell her that I wish he'd just stay there forever. But when I get there, I notice that Nicole is even quieter than usual. She looks tired and keeps checking her phone. We both don't really say anything until we find a bench and sit down before the boardwalk. A few sparrows flit by, and one clutches a dead reed that managed to stand over the worst of winter.

"We aren't meant to be creatures who ruin everything," she says, eyes locked on the bird.

"You been reading?"

"Ha, yeah. *Braiding Sweetgrass*. She talks about how grass that has been tended to, has been harvested, is the healthiest grass. Like mowing a lawn. The scientist who studied it said all the Western scientists didn't think the hypothesis was even worth testing. But then she came back with her findings, and it was true. The grass needed human touch to be its best."

"It's a nice thought. Though I think we've probably screwed with it more than we've helped it."

"I don't know. Maybe some of us."

"I guess my grandpa has always treated the earth pretty well. He has a place up north, and he gardens every year. It does seem like the plants do better and better. Well, when I was little enough to go more often." I stop myself, realizing I am saying too much.

"You don't go anymore?"

"Just busier, I guess."

I try to change the subject, but a stupid question comes out. "What happened to the other guy you were dating? The one on your Instagram?"

She laughs and leans her head back on the bench. "We tried to stay together, you know, when I moved." She looks at the sky. "But I messed that up."

"I don't see that. What happened?"

She looks over at me. "I wasn't exactly 'honest.'"

I nod. "You miss him?" I grab a dead leaf off the ground and spin it in my fingers.

"Yeah." She looks out at the frozen lake. "We met as freshman and had been dating for almost a year. He moved to Minneapolis from Fond du Lac. We got to know each other pretty fast." She smiles. "When you're both Anishinaabe, you skip a whole lot." I can imagine. To have someone know so much of you already.

"We once went to visit his mom up in Fond du Lac. She was so cool, a social worker like my dad. And Aaron wants to be in the sciences. Help his tribe with things, too."

"Do you think he's missing you back?"

"He might. I don't know. We don't really talk anymore, to make it easier. We were still together when I moved." She looks down at her mittens. "Then I was just missing him and missing everything, was sad, and it was rough."

"That how Luca and you got together?"

"Yeah, I guess, though I don't think I've ever stopped having feelings for Luca. He came and visited me when he was in the cities for a soccer tournament in the fall. So we kinda started talking again after that." She rubs her arm. "And then I was lonely over the holidays just being here with Mom and no one else, and we went out to catch up, and we just, you know. There was a lot of emotions, and before we knew it, we just went there. And I screwed it up. I guess sometimes doors open and close at the same time."

She continues. "I think Aaron was hooking up with someone else right after we broke up because of something I saw online. They were flirting in the comments somewhere. And that's fine, I guess. Like, I can't judge. Before all this, we had planned to try to stay together, but now—"

"No waiting for each other?"

"What would we be waiting for?" She stares upward again. "I don't know. Maybe we'll both end up at the University of Minnesota," she says, like she's already thought of it. And her words give me some hope.

"Not that I'd ever say that to Luca." She sighs and then turns to look at me. "Well, what about you, Jay?" she asks. "Any girls catching your eye?"

I laugh at her question. "Sure. But I don't really think I'm in the place to date anyone. It's, like, hard to crush on girls. Like, everyone is just a little freaked out by Max and me right now."

"I guess I can see that." She laughs. "Maybe I need to find you someone from Minneapolis. A bunch of my friends all thought you were super hot when I showed them a photo of my cousins who lived here."

"Really?" I forgot these are the things people tell each other. And it's nice, I guess.

"Come on, Jay. Look at you. You're, like, all extra now, with your long hair, all this lean muscle. Tall. Like, who are you?"

I laugh. "I don't know." I wrap my arms around myself as a cold breeze pushes by.

"I think you are figuring it out." Nicole's eyes look genuine, and she bumps her shoulder into mine.

We sit and watch the birds, and I wish I could do more of these kinds of afternoons. I am grateful she's shared so much of herself with me. I wish I could give back. But what does my world, my dad, my family offer?

DINNER

We don't know who we are when I get home. We don't know how to act with one another. Max can't look at me. If Dad were here, Max knows it would have been his shift to watch Mom for the last couple of days, and in the habit, he's still near her, doing his homework when I come down the stairs.

I sit next to him at the kitchen island, and he hides a sketch from me. But I see a flash of red ink. I know he probably regrets leaving Mom the other day. I'm still frustrated. I am the one who got Dad to leave, the one who finally laid him out, the only muscle to meet Dad's. The only one even trying to participate in counseling. I want to be so upset at Max, but why ruin these two days? I have to honor the freedom we never get.

Instead, I start running water for the dishes while Mom cooks. We have a working dishwasher, but Dad wants us to wash by hand and has shown us a million times how to wash a dish right.

I watch Mom. Each of her movements are timed so every part of the meal comes out *hot*. Less salt. The chicken just as he likes it.

Dad is still here even when he isn't. I set the table and, when we all finally sit, the whole meal is just as calculated. We even wait for him to take the pepper first. We obey his rules. No elbows on the table. No talking other than to ask how the day went. We sit quietly after answering one another because he needs silence after a long day of work.

Should we enjoy it, the freedom behind this discomfort? Is it freedom if it will all end in another day?

ROOFS

Dad's construction company has had him in so many places remodeling and rebuilding. Recently, in Bemidji, other times just in office buildings in town. But the one I think of most often is his first site repairing roofs for suburban homes just outside town. The houses all fall apart at the same time out there. A large housing development where each house was built at the same time will, in ten years and six months, become a cul-de-sac squalling with needs. Dad thrived on the seasonal decay. He used to take us to his new jobsites to show us how hard he was working. He would tether his body to the roof to keep steady, and then he would replace square foot by square foot of roofing. He shouted down at us for nails, and we'd climb a tall ladder to take him what he needed. He seemed to like having power. One demand from him was one quick action from us. We bustled below at fifteen, picking up items for him and watching him rain down torn-up, mossy shingles onto a black tarp below.

He'd stand on those roofs and look out across the tops of those communities like he owned them, take a swig from his flask. I remember he once yelled, "Damn, I'm on the top of the tallest house, and it still doesn't give me much!"

His foreman yelled at him from another roof, "Stop fucking around, Tobias."

Dad flinched the smallest bit; I still remember the centimeter. He swore and yelled at us to get our asses into gear and get him a different hammer from his truck. Wasn't much like the dad who used to check our seat belts twice, then give us a poke on the cheek. If he could see himself today, if he really got a good look, I think the man he was would apologize. The better man.

DAY THREE

"Someone used my fucking truck. There are fifty more miles on it."

Max holds his breath. Dad is back from his few days at the precinct.

My internal sigh. Did Max take his truck?

Mom is about to open her mouth, but before she does, he pours down words. Out of the side of his eye, I see him glance at my crossed arms. He won't lay a hand on me. I think, *Go ahead, take a good look.* He swears at me because I've made my move. I've flipped the dynamics. He knows he can't kick me out because I help with the rent. He grabs his keys, a set or two of work clothes, a blanket, and a few movies. Back to the basement.

HALF OF IT

Max isn't here for our next meeting with Luca. I'm only half surprised. He's been missing everything lately. Though he made it to our session on Monday.

I call him, but he isn't answering. I've been faithfully doing our counseling homework this week. Cutting out anything about our family. Ms. Hannan had us write about our extended family and their responses to the difficulties they went through. What is she going to know about kinship, about our distance from our family? We were always too poor to go visit Costa Rica. I journaled about this separately, and I didn't bring it to our session. I also wrote about how I love Max and would die for him, but lately he's left me fixing stuff *every time*. It's been me caring about Mom. Me working, me calling Max, while he is off doing his art all the time. I would like to get to do something, to dream. Even Nicole, a year behind us, is getting to plan for college at the University of Minnesota.

Luca must be sitting outside the room, because I can see his counselor through the window looking down and talking.

Ms. Hannan is trying not to look at me, but I can see her evaluating the situation each time I call. No answer.

"Dammit, Max," I say. All this is for him anyway. I'm coming here to show we've done reconciliation after we beat up Luca. It's to show a shiny new record to MCAD. I look at Ms. Hannan, who is now sipping a hot mug of tea.

"Can this be done any other day?" I ask her.

"Ideally, we'd have you all here today."

"Can't I just do it?" I ask. She sighs.

"Let me talk to his counselor."

LUCA

His counselor agrees, and it's Luca and me sitting across from each other. The counselors in chairs at each of our right hands.

"Luca has a few things he'd like to say," the counselor says, looking at Luca encouragingly.

"Well, I know Nicole and I were both upset, and I didn't mean for anything to happen. I was never going to do anything. But that's not a reason for you to do what you did."

His counselor seems surprised at his last sentence. I am quiet for a moment and nod. I try to be a little empathetic. I think of Nicole and how we all have our pieces of who we are. But I think about how Nicole didn't deserve what he did, no matter what his issues are. I think about what I'd want from my own father—to really trust him again.

"Nicole didn't deserve what you did. Can you admit that?" Luca's eyes get defensive. His counselor looks over to him to see what he'll say. "Can you at least admit that you messed up, too?" I say.

"I respect Nicole," Luca says, his eyes zeroing in on me.

"If you do care about Nicole, it seems like you'd try to do more to make it work." It sounds like a threat. But I am composed.

"Listen, Nicole has got her own stuff. We're working through it."

The way he doesn't fess up is making me mad, though.

"If you remember right, you and your brother were the ones who beat me up," Luca says, sitting up straight. "I am the victim here. It's lucky I had time to heal before college soccer season or this would have ruined my life."

"I'm sorry I didn't ruin your life more," I say sarcastically.

"Okay! Well, we have more to do," his counselor says, closing her notebook, looking at my counselor. They must be making a silent agreement, because they share a hard but friendly nod. Then Luca's counselor says something that sounds practical but still cuts me. "Let's meet again when Max is ready." I tighten my fist under the cover of my chair.

Luca grabs his backpack in a fast swipe. His counselor is the first to walk out. "Watch yourself, Jay," he says in a softness under his breath with his back to my counselor, and leaves quickly. He must have not thought that Ms. Hannan was paying attention, but she saw whatever look is on my face.

I look at her after the door closes. "See, he hasn't changed."

She breathes. "Okay, Jay. I get it. But you need to grow here, too. You can't just go and beat up people when things go wrong. And you can't control their actions, either."

"I know. It's not like I was going to go off on him. I wanted to see if he'd apologize."

"But you've just threatened him all over again. Did you see that?"

"I guess."

"So you're not above any of this. No one is."

IV

MAX

...

We go to the movies. I take Mom's car
to the old theater, across town,
far from the 7-Eleven, far from
home right after school.

The red and yellow-orange
exterior lights flash in a firefly frenzy.
She picked a vintage showing.

I didn't mean for my time
with Melody to hurt Mom
the week before. I dropped off her painting,
and we got a coffee and talked for so long.

I wonder how people leave, how they
have it all. How all those artists
with homes like mine could
even step out without hurting anyone?
They make their own dwellings, like Grandpa's in
the northern woods, of peace.

...

…
Does Mom know what
it feels like to hold someone's hand?

Does she even remember what
it's like to have someone ask how you are?

Do I even know this is real?
I'm dizzy when Melody
leans on my shoulder with hers.

Did I know that someone could ask
what I'm thinking, and I could honestly
say, *I'm having a really good time.*
…

…

I've always been safe from Dad in my art.
When someone cares only about themselves,
they don't make time for what you love.

Maybe this is how God keeps it safe just
for me. Dad's never asked to see.

Never wanted to look. Never
wanted to even care.
Art wasn't a threat to him.
Not something to him worth
controlling. Even though if he did
take one moment to look, he'd
see that he is all over it.

…

…

Melody says she'll text me tonight
when we leave the theater.
I ask her if she wants to
keep getting together.

She says, *Of course.*
You just said you had a good time?

I say, *Yeah, I did.*

I feel guilty for hiding and going home. The danger of Jay
is that he *cares*. We've never had secrets from each other,
how we've always done it.
But I am not willing to share this,
all this joy is too good to lose with Jay
calling it selfish like he seems to think about me
going to school, about me leaving, me making
time for art. I can already see that in
him. And with Melody?

I want this place to be all mine and
Melody's.

…

…

Would you mind if we keep things quiet?
I just don't know if I want Jay to know right now, I ask.

I can. I don't love secrets, she says. *But sure.*

I know if she did love secrets, this already wouldn't work.
I wouldn't be as safe as I am.

…

...

I turn my phone back on, and I see all of Jay's calls and text messages. I dread having to be in counseling with him, keeping this secret.

I call Ms. Hannan, apologize for missing our session with Luca, and ask if Jay and I can do our personal meeting separately.

She agrees. I say I will be at the next group reconciliation and will see her on Wednesday.

But at least now—when Jay has his sessions—unquestioned freedom for me for an hour after school.

...

V

JAY

BACKYARD

I text Max that he needs to stay home before I leave for work on Saturday. I ask him if wherever he's been going can wait. I see that he read it. A few moments later.

MAX: Of course. No problem.

When I get home from work early Saturday evening, the living room is empty. A stack of dirty dishes is in the sink. A little painting of an orange sunset that Max did is perched on the open shelf. We are in a strange warm front for mid-February. He must have painted in the backyard today. A happy medium. I hear his music coming from his bedroom. We can do this. I go to the dishes, pull my sleeves up. In the back of my head, I hear Dad's voice chiding Mom for these being in the sink. When I pull back the curtain for natural light, I see her in the backyard with her legs up on the long lawn chair. She is petting the neighbor's dog and looking at our vacant garden. Her fingers unspool over the dog's ears.

When I finish the dishes, I go out to her. The dog grumbles at me and walks back to her yard. "It was just one time, Molly," I say. "I'm sorry."

Mom, who usually would have laughed at this, continues to stare out at the yard, her hands now crossed over her soft midsection.

"Want to watch anything? Saw a couple of new things for cheap on streaming," I ask her.

She sighs and doesn't look at me. "Save your money, Jay."

"For what?" I ask her.

"For something other than me," she says.

MAX'S STUDIO

To be jealous of a studio, a painting, it's ridiculous. But my drive to complete anything has disappeared since Dad returned from his two-day vacation. I've even skipped working out a few days because I'm down to just thinking of Mom, even after Nicole and I've grown a little closer. I know better than to do this when I am feeling this way, but I try to avoid Nicole on Monday, which isn't too hard because she and Luca sometimes leave campus for lunch. I go by Max's studio in the high-ceilinged school art room.

Max isn't there since it isn't his lunch hour, but his paintings stop me—they are huge, dark, and daunting. He has moved on from the layers of color one on top of the other. These have shape and seem alive. One is of a vivid green river. He's even rubbed cottonwood seeds onto the canvas. The Mississippi catches the seeds like that. They get splayed out with the touch of water, finding their full selves. The other one that wraps the corner of the room is very dark. It's a storm, I think, with lots of gray, red, purple, and blue, too. It looks dangerous and uncontrollable. There is also a small portrait of our Bribri relatives. A picture Grandpa used to show us of his sisters and brothers. Instead of being in that sepia color, though, they are surrounded by green palms and yellow fruit, a light blue sky. I stand in front of that one for a while. He has Post-its labeling which ones he's putting in his application portfolio. Maybe I am not jealous of his studio. I am jealous of his living. Even when I am standing here breathing, how ridiculous.

AFTER CHURCH

On Sunday after the service, I wait in the car while Mom and Dad talk to a few people and Max helps the volunteers clean up. I don't want to be around anyone today. I look out the window, and I see one of Nicole's mom's for-sale signs in the yard of a brick house.

The house is lit up with leftover-Christmas lights. I see Shelly walk out in a petticoat and leather boots and shove into the frozen lawn an open-house sign with an arrow pointing at the door. I smile, thinking of how Shelly doesn't let anything get in her way. Even a cold lawn. In another minute, Luca's dad's Jeep rolls up. I see Nicole and Luca in the front seat. Nicole looks upset. It looks like she is trying to explain something to him sternly, her body turned toward him. Luca is shaking his head at her like someone does with a child. His posture is defensive now, and then he's talking with his hands and gesturing at her like she's being ridiculous. Nicole, who hardly ever looks small, gets small. His head shaking even more and an eye roll.

Shelly pops her head out the front door and waves at the two of them. Luca sees her right away, and his expression morphs into a smile that would fool me. The kind boyfriend. Nicole squares her shoulders, folds down the mirror, puts on dark red lipstick and sunglasses, and steps out of the car before Luca does. Whatever he just told her couldn't be good.

MATH TEACHER VISITS COUNSELOR'S OFFICE

"You know how to do this stuff, Jay. You're good at math," my calculus teacher, Ms. Johnson, says.

Ms. Hannan has brought her to our session. The green chair next to mine where Max is supposed to sit is frayed even worse than the one I am sitting on.

"Maybe cut down on your work hours or cut out other distractions?" Ms. Johnson suggests.

"What's wrong with experimenting?" I ask. I have begun writing questions about the relevance of each problem. I can solve them in less than a minute, but I am tired of spitting out answers for her. Couldn't we learn how to build an unbreakable bridge or how to purify our polluted rivers? I could tell her about how the layers of the Bribri universe mimics the planets, how sweetgrass grows better with us humans.

"Can't you just do it right on one sheet and turn it in? Keep the other for your own sake?" Ms. Johnson asks.

"You say to show your work," I say. "I'm working out the meaning."

"Do you want to go to college?"

"Haven't thought about it," I lie. I have, over and over again, but I could never leave home. Even if Dad lived in the basement for the rest of his life. The only thing nearby is a two-year college. And that wasn't what I wanted. I'm never getting what Grandpa has—the degrees upon degrees.

She sighs. "Just do it right on the front and do whatever other work you want to on the back, and I'll pass you. You've been on the honor roll your entire high school career, Jay. You don't want to give that up."

Ms. Hannan nods in agreement, her hands clasped together on her desk. When Ms. Johnson leaves, Ms. Hannan asks, "Everything okay, Jay?" I don't answer, put my backpack on, and leave her office.

When I get home, I tear off the honor roll sticker on the right side of Dad's bumper.

At least Max is home in time.

NEXT DAY

I avoid seeing anyone. I eat in the library corner. My old calc group studies in the nearby computer lab. I avoid where I usually run into Nicole in the hallways. And when I'm finally heading out the front doors after the final bell rings us into another gray day, I feel a hand on my shoulder, and I go cold. Luca's face flashes in my mind. But that wouldn't make sense, not in front of everyone here.

I turn around, and Nicole is behind me on the front steps. "Where have you been?"

She stands up straight, shoulders back.

"I figured you'd want to enjoy your lunch with Luca," I say.

"Not really. We're fighting again." She rolls her eyes. I realize I forgot about seeing Luca and her over the weekend.

"Oh right. Yeah, I saw you guys in front of your mom's showing on Sunday," I say.

"Yeah?" She crosses her arms.

"You guys fighting a lot, a lot?"

"I thought I'd lay down some boundaries. But he didn't like that." She steps down from her upper step and walks ahead of me.

"He's a real ass," I say, and maybe it comes out loud enough for a few students to look back at me.

"Tell me about it." She keeps walking. I sigh and catch up to her.

"So what's the new thing? What was it about?" I ask.

"Well, he doesn't like that you and I hang out. But from the start, I told him I don't cut out family, because that's happened enough in my own life. When we moved with Dad, I hardly saw you guys. Not anyone's fault, just situational. And I don't want that anymore. Luca can get over it. He thinks you are trying to break us up."

"Well, I—"

"Like it matters what you want. This is my life." She breathes hard and pulls out her phone. "I have to ask my mom for a ride today. He said he couldn't take me."

"I'm sorry," I say.

"Yeah, me too," she says, then puts her phone up to her ear. "Mom, can you get me?" They talk for a few seconds. "No, Luca couldn't. Yeah. Bye." Nicole hangs up.

I wait with her, and we're awkwardly quiet for a bit. I guess I'm grateful she stood up for me. I try to think of something to say. I think about how much I hated seeing my calc group studying together. They all looked like they were having such a good time.

"Hey, so I'm behind on homework. Would you want to come over in a couple of days, and we can do work together or something?" I ask.

"Oh heck yes. Happy to help, if you need. I'd love to see your mom, too," Nicole says, grinning.

Of course she'd say she wants to see my mom. In a few more minutes, Shelly pulls up in her maroon SUV. She has on her glitzy sunglasses and a big poufy black jacket, and her hair is back in a ponytail. She rolls down her window, leans over the seat, and yells, "So good to see you, Jay! My goodness you are growing up. My handsome nephew!"

"See? Growing up." Nicole raises her eyebrows at me and points at her mom behind her.

"Hi, Shelly." I wave at her.

"Be good!" She waves back. Nicole hops into the car and waves. I laugh a little.

And they are gone in a flash.

MEATBALLS

Dad makes meatballs, and we all eat at the table quietly. Max is in a whole other world, smiling while he eats. And I don't know what the hell is going on. When we finish, Dad thanks me for buying the groceries. I want to lay him out right there. Or string him up on the clothesline where Mom spends more time than she needs to. We all spend more time out than we need to. Dinner is our only time together. I don't want him to die. But a little pain wouldn't hurt.

Something close.

HOMEWORK

Nicole comes over after school a few days later, and when I open the door, I see she has a big scarf on shielding her from the cold wind.

"Welcome!" I say. She half smiles.

"Let's get you caught up." She comes in and looks around like she wants to see something new but is disappointed. Then she puts her bag down and starts unlacing her black leather boots.

Mom comes from upstairs and is surprised to see Nicole at the door, but she gives her a big hug. I see my cousin scrutinize Mom's face. She's not anywhere near the Christmas Mom Nicole saw every year. Mom and she talk for a little bit and get caught up while I put some hot water on for tea. It's been a long time since we've had a guest.

I spread out my homework on the kitchen island. It's a mess. In a few minutes, Nicole is over, adjusting her glasses. "God, you are behind."

I laugh. We sit down, and we sort through everything. It helps me more than she knows. I start while she finishes her assignments for the night within a half hour, then begins reading *Braiding Sweetgrass*. I file away my completed equations and pull out my science textbook.

"So Max decided to meet separately with our counselor," I say, looking over a worksheet. "He's probably tired of me."

"I don't think that's true," she says, putting down the book just slightly. "Probably needs his own space. I mean, Jay, you two are, like, about to be done with high school. Gotta grow those wings."

I roll my eyes. "Yeah, but now he's not showing up for the joint sessions with Luca. And the whole—or I mean, part of—the reason

I'm doing it is because he's wanting to get into art school. But, like, if he can't show up, I have no idea what school would be down for that. He's losing time. February is almost over, and the April deadline is going to be here soon."

Nicole laughs. "You can't do it all for him, Jay."

I get up and reheat my tea. In one sitting, I complete my homework from the last two weeks. I write a paper on Western plot structure in Shakespeare's *Hamlet* for Honors English, have Nicole look it over. (She says it's fine, boring, but fine.)

"You need to read more. Like outside of class," she says, frowning at my paper.

"I know, I know."

I want to learn more about Bribri story structures. But I can't think about that right now. I have to do each project the way the teacher wants, on their given topics, but what does a grade mean? That I get to do another grade after this? And then what? The world for me is not as wide as it seemed on the *Empire Builder* when Max and I were kids. But I do all my homework and makeup-work anyway.

"So have things gotten better? With Luca?" And I'm surprised I'm being genuine. But she's my cousin and I trust her. Like, for real.

"I don't know. He's having a hard time. Worried about his own scholarships. Stressed out. But honestly, I'm a little tired of it."

"Sure. I can understand that."

I look at the kitchen clock and realize Dad is coming back in ten minutes.

"Hey, Nicole, it's getting late. Is it okay if you head out?"

She has a pencil in her mouth, her focus on another book from her bag. "Yeah, for sure." She looks at her phone. "I guess I probably could help my mom with dinner."

She takes some time putting away her things. And I watch the clock, worried he'll come through the door. She pulls her backpack over her shoulder, puts her boots on, and then touches my hand.

"Shaking." She says it like a statement. Her eyes look right into mine.

"It's nothing."

"Whatever you say." And she's out the door with two minutes to spare.

ART OF NOTHING

I would never say this to Max—but when I see him bring home his paintings on the weekends, I try to imagine if I had painted them. I have no energy for the stories I used to write. Math doesn't come to mind whenever I think about the formation of the earth. I've tried to sketch in one of those small, lined notebooks that we sell at the gas station, but my drawings are terrible. I draw the bench, but no one can look into my mind and understand it. No one can see me missing my brother in each wobbly line of graphite. No one can see Dad in the wooden splinters.

The art is not there.

I've heard that you can do art anywhere, but really, I miss experiencing it for myself. I was going to skip the Honors English field trip, but at the last minute, I ask Mom to sign the permission slip to go see *Richard III*. I pay the extra fifteen-dollar late fee myself because I'm desperate.

Max can paint his room over and over again if he wants to. And he does. His room is full of various people smudged onto canvases. He has still lifes all reimagined in paint—green books, red vases, the like. Each one, unlike my bench sketch, embedded heavily with so much more. Blue and pulsing reds. He seems to have found hope.

FIELD TRIP

Juniors and seniors in Honors English get into two buses to head to the cities for a matinee showing of *Richard III* at the Guthrie. I see Nicole get on one bus with Luca, and I try to pass it by to sit on the other bus, but our English teacher, Ms. Constant, stops me.

"Let's go, Jay," she says from her clipboard, her back to the open door. "You're on this bus." I turn around and sigh.

"You're not getting out of this," she says.

"Wouldn't dream of it," I say, and step up the stairs.

"Why don't you sit in the front with me?" she says. "Front row, behind the driver." Great. Even one of my favorite teachers doesn't trust me.

I get on the bus and see Luca next to Nicole. His sunny smile disappears when he sees me. Nicole notices it right away, brushes his shoulder, and shakes her head at him. His eyes turn to fire for a second at her. I turn around before I do anything I don't want to. I'm already causing something. I sling my backpack onto my lap, and my legs are so long that they are hiked up in the seat.

Ms. Constant stands next to me, accounting for each student.

The drive is two and a half hours, and I watch the end of winter out the window. Flurries skim past us. Some places have lost their snow, and it's just bitter-looking. Gray grass, frosted hay, barren trees. Ms. Constant is on her phone, quiet. Then we get to the suburbs and then the cities. We pull onto Washington Avenue in downtown Minneapolis where the city begins with old brick buildings. Art centers, studio spaces. Salons.

"Did you like our Shakespeare unit?" Ms. Constant asks.

I nod. "I like it all. We haven't read *Richard III*, so I'm looking forward to it."

"I think you'll like it," she says.

THE GUTHRIE

The theater isn't in a historic building; it's dark blue, glassed, and modern. Pushed in various geometric directions. A section of it looks like a blue bridge to nowhere suspended toward the river. Another room extends from the upper floors and is lit up yellow. A huge portrait of a man is suspended on one of the entrance walls. We're told that we have time to explore after the show and that we'll be getting lunch delivered.

Light snow is coming down as we walk through the front doors and get in a long line in front of the ticket table they set up for schools. I try not to spot Luca and Nicole again, but I see them talking around a corner near the gift shop. I hear Nicole say in a frustrated voice, "Why do you have to look at him that way?"

"We've gone over this so much, Nicole. You were there. You saw them go crazy on me." I don't know what to do. But I know I can't do anything. I can't.

"It wasn't like they responded for nothing."

"So you are on their side?"

"I don't want to take sides."

"You need to stop being a—"

I bite my lip. The heat rises in my chest.

The teller coughs. "Your ticket?"

I look up and the ticket and playbill are in a gloved hand. "Thanks."

I take it and am guided up a thin escalator. Classmates get on behind me, and I look back. The escalator has already pulled me out of their sight. Luca can't do anything here. He isn't going to flip out. Not with so many people around.

RICHARD III

I linger around the beverage bar, waiting for an extra minute, hoping Nicole will come up the escalator. But then I figure maybe it wouldn't be good if I was there right after they argued. I walk into the red velvet auditorium. The seating surrounds a dark stage. The set design has mirrors, steps, and a ladder lit with purple and blue. I sit down in the third tier where nearly the rest of the classes are. No one paid attention to their seat numbers and are sitting with friends, so I slip in on an end where there's lots of room.

I look through the playbill, read the designer notes and director's statement about how this play is a conversation about power, the intrigue of evil, the way our words are means of violence, and how these themes don't seem so far from contemporary politics and life. The casting is diverse, and I read through a few folks' bios before I sense someone next to me.

"Can I sit with you?" It's Nicole, and I nod. Music has begun to play in the background, and the lights dim.

"Thanks." I can hear her breathing as she takes off her jacket and places it on the ground. When she sits down, I lean over. "Everything okay?"

Her eyes are glossy. "Well, we're done," she says.

"You and Luca?"

She looks at the playbill. "I've given him enough chances. Now let's watch this damn play."

I don't know how to respond, but I want to give her a hug. We sit back, and my chest pounds like I've run a race, but it isn't even mine. She's braver than I am. Like always.

WHEN SOMEONE CHANGES BUT YOU'RE NOT SURE IF YOU WANTED THEM TO

When I get home from the show, from it all, I can't help but be relieved. I even think about the religious charade that Richard played up in the show and how it reminded me of Luca at school, all his volunteer work, his mentoring. But more so, it makes me think of Dad at church. And it makes me think about how you can go only so far. The actor was sweaty by the end of the night; even acting as a villain is exhausting.

Mom tells me that Pastor learned about Dad's time in jail. And I don't think he is surprised. He knows us. Dad is not the best fake, and the thing about Pastor is that he could probably always see it, even in Dad's easy frustration about something as simple as the coffee going cold after church. Maybe he's seen stuff like this, too.

Pastor asked Dad to meet him at his office after work. Dad gets home a few hours later than he usually does. And over the week, Dad makes us breakfast early in the morning, he buys us the tennis shoes we needed last year. He brings flowers home for Mom and says thank you for dinner.

And then I lay him out when he drinks too much and goes after Mom again. He lands one fist on her, and I turn him into a cold ice cube on the floor.

I pull him out to the front steps, lock the doors, put only his car keys on his lap. After a while, I hear his truck rev up. I pray that he's leaving for a long, long time. I ice my hands, and the ache is there through the night.

MOVIE NIGHT

Max and I lie on top of the blanket of Mom's bed, one of us on either side of her. We watch *A Good Year*, her favorite movie. I made a bowl of popcorn.

I can't look away from her cheek still blotting in the oblong shapes of grapefruit flesh. After a while, she's got an arm around each of us. Her sweet fingers spindle the hair that has grown down past my neck and shoulders. I hear her kiss Max's forehead.

WALK

Mom is sitting on the couch the next morning. Her black hair, streaked with silver, lies against the back cushion. No breakfast has been made. She has her own new tennis shoes on and a zip-up hoodie. She's staring at the wall.

"He's going to stay at Pastor's," she says. "For a month."

"Did you tell him what happened?"

"He doesn't know about the—" she stops. "The hitting. He just thinks he needs some time to grow." I can't believe she said it aloud. We've never said what he's done. But I don't want to make a big thing of it.

"Are you going somewhere?" I ask, pointing at her shoes.

"I was thinking of a walk," she says. Max stares at her with wide eyes.

"Mom, you okay?" I ask, sitting on the coffee table across from her.

"I hear sometimes it's good to go on a walk when you're sad," she says.

"I think it can be," I say. "Should we?"

"Sure, hun."

We walk around a few blocks. Mom and me.

LIBRARY

"Another wall?" Nicole says, looking at my hand on Monday. Ms. Hannan lets me skip counseling to take the ACT after school today with one of the community classes. Nicole sits with me to wait in the library.

"Yeah."

"Maybe you should stop hitting walls?" she suggests as she glances down at a stack of books she has sitting next to her. On the top, another one the librarian ordered for her.

"I'll see what I can do," I say.

Nicole sighs and lies back on the floor, her arms out. "You know, I feel free. I really do."

"That must be pretty nice," I say.

"It is. It really is."

I would love to be free. To find a way. I look at this bruised fist. I don't know if there is a way.

"You're gonna kick ass on this test," she says.

"I don't know about that."

"You are. You really are."

ACT

Please fill in your answers completely.

What is the smallest common denominator of 42, 126, and 210?
2.

Which of the following statements about the meteorite craters on Europa would be the most consistent with both scientists' views?
  A. *No meteorites have struck Europa for millions of years.*
  B. *Meteorite craters, once formed, are then smoothed or removed by Europa's surface process.*
  C. *Meteorite craters, once formed on Europa, remain unchanged for billions of years.*
  D. *Meteorites frequently strike Europa's surface but do not leave any craters.*

B.

He is waiting by the back door.
Choose the best answer.
  A. *No change.*
  B. *He is waiting, by the back door.*
  C. *He, is waiting by the back door.*

A.

Ten days later, I get a letter in the mail. I got a thirty-one.

LIGHT

Max and I come home from school together for the first time in a long time, and a cord is in the socket outside the bathroom leading under the door. Max doesn't think about it as he steps over the cord. I freeze.

I yell at the door.

Mom answers, annoyed.

The light in the bathroom was too bright for a bath, so she brought in a lamp.

WEDNESDAY COUNSELING

Mom calls me, *Jay, blue jay*, when the blue jays return to nest in our backyard. When she sings it again, I remember how mean those birds are. How they chase other birds if they try to take food, how they shout and scream. Mom says they're beautiful. She loves their color. Their babies peek their heads out, gray and fuzzy, while their wings and legs bleed blue, still stuck in the nest.

I don't know why, but I actually tell my counselor that story. I say I am worried about my mom. It's the first time I've told her anything, and she just listens. Maybe it's easier if Max isn't here.

"Do you think your concern for your mom causes you to be upset about anything?"

I shrug. She gives me an assignment to spend a little time writing. "It might help you prepare to talk with Luca next time." There is no way in hell I want to talk to Luca. Not after he and Nicole broke up. I realize that some part of me was trying because Nicole was trying. Not anymore.

"Is Max going to be there?" I ask. She says she can't make that decision for him. She has to report progress. The word *progress* makes me sick. Max's deadline is so soon. I already avoid all of Luca's regular hallway routes. I've managed to not see him again since the theater. Nicole and I requested to sit on the other bus on the way home, and Ms. Constant agreed.

NORMALCY

Grandpa Fernando comes to stay with us, and it hits me that we haven't seen him for two years. His wrinkles are a little deeper, oily and joyful. He gives us hugs and a kiss on the head. He grips Mom's hand extra hard as if to remind her he's here. He takes his suitcase upstairs, despite our offering. And when he returns, he has a beetle, the invasive red beetle, an early sign of spring in his thick hands, and carries it outside. It isn't a soft move, though. It's sacred. I drag my bed into Max's room. We set up a bed frame and mattress we had stored in the basement that we used to set up when he'd come visit us.

They need normalcy; that's what Pastor said.

Our grandpa does not say too much while he gets settled in. I can hear him humming a Bribri lullaby I recognize. Already, the whole world sings of normalcy with Grandpa here. Even the bugs come out at night. They are there singing and fighting all the time. For song's sake, for sex's sake, for death's sake, for life's sake. I don't know why I could never hear them from other springs before. How much of all this has been taken from us? What is it worth now?

ROOMMATES

Max and I sleep in the same room, and, even now, I hardly see him. He's taken to staying at the art studio after school for hours. He shows up only to eat, looking happier than ever—but never shares about his day other than to say *good*. He leaves for school early in the morning, too, so he can prep his canvases, he says. He doesn't talk much about painting, either; he just does it. And I miss him. Our home has been cracked open, and when the only thing that might bring us closer happens—Dad gone—now it's Max.

He, too, is gone.

VI

MAX

…

I try to hide that I'm not happy
with it. I don't want to look at it,

so I turn it away to dry. Melody has
leaned back into the beanbag
in the school's studio. A big book in her hand
of photography prints.

I take some time to gather
my paints into my backpack.

Among them, I find a few smooth stones,
lots of leaves I picked up on one of our walks.

I place them on my easel for ideation.
I'll practice their shapes later.
Grandpa asked me if I was interested in sculpture,
and I have begun experimenting even more than
the cottonwood. His knowledge of art gently deep
from his degrees.
I know to listen.

…

…
When I get home
after school,

Jay's on the couch,
eyes at the ceiling.

He blends in,
and for a moment

it makes me sick.
I want to push him off

the couch—dare him
to do *something*.
…

...
Grandpa is
sitting at the
kitchen island.

He lifts his head
at me in greeting.

And this is how

they look

                    two

              islands,

                    but one island has
                    become almost
                    ...

n

o

t

h

i

n

g.

Grandpa,
why haven't you asked
him to do anything?
Wouldn't it help him?
But I don't say
the words.

…
For eight to twelve dollars,
I can buy canvases and
plastic sheets from Walmart.

I tell Mom,
an easy forty dollars.

She nods, gives me cash,
but she nods like she would
when Dad asked her for anything.

Here we are
without Dad home,
and here she still is.

I want to give it back,
but I already told Melody
I'd take her to dinner since her parents
can't ever really give her money. And
I don't want to start making
empty promises.
…

...
I think of what
Jay and I would have done
on a free day. But
Jay has family, Nicole.

She's been hanging out with him,
watching after him. Her
and Luca apart.

Taking my place.

I get it. I want it.

Less for me to do.
...

…
But even I see Nicole
is angry
at me
when I pass her
at school.

Like I've left
my people.

And I can already hear her saying
you have.

But my people
are in my art. They only
hurt me as much as I let
them.
…

…
I don't get why we have to sneak around,
Melody says.
I can't explain that
I have never lied to Jay
except about her.

And if I told him the truth,
I couldn't stand how he'd look at me.
Like Nicole just did, but worse.
Like I've left my family behind,
for some art and a high school romance.

I am not wanting him to drag me
down with him. Stopping life
because of home.

I already feel him doing that with my art.
How can I create at a time like this?
How much more would he be betrayed
if he knew everything?
…

...

On the weekdays, I leave home early
to get to school right at
six a.m. and paint for a few hours.

I tuck away my frustration from Melody. Here
alone in the studio—I can be upset.

I paint my emotions toward Mom. My
questions—why has she let this go on so long?
Even at Grandpa, for not doing more.

I paint someone stuck to a couch. Then I paint
grip marks that used to be on my arms like tattoos,
like a print—I become the jaguar.

The pattern mine to have now. Here, wounds
to art, in my paint skin memory. I sit and watch it dry.

I watch as each color
hardens on the canvas. I see it's good already.
A key project for my portfolio.
The April deadline is coming soon to claim it.

...

VII
JAY

THE MARKET OF TLATELOLCO

In my old room, Grandpa unpacks all his suitcases. Suits and ties and lots of books settle into corners. He puts his record player in the living room, and in his room, he puts his radio on my dresser. It is set to some historical station that talks about scientific findings, discourse around philosophy, and on occasion a BBC roundup of world current events. "I will decide myself what I think," he says. He listens to the radio while he reads the paper in the chair he moved in with; his one braid behind his back, and his bolo-collared shirt ironed. On a small table he set near his chair, I see that Mom has made hot chocolate just for him. Something she hasn't made for us in a long time.

He offers me his books. I pick out one on geometry, another on art history. I start reading the heavy art book on the floor, and Grandpa and I sit undisturbed. As I flip the pages, I'm trying to understand Max. I try to look deeply into each painting for something that would make me understand him. Some sign. I look for the bold colors he uses now—the reds, blues, and blacks I've seen on his pants in the laundry room. There are some paintings like his. They remind me of violence. But even the Picassos look a little violent, those eyes and jaws in every which way. A bloodied Christ makes me suck in my breath. And yet the bios of the artists leave me wanting. They tell me only location, parentage, heritage, name.

Grandpa hands me another book on Latin American murals and smaller painting collections. Details on the complicated love lives of Diego Rivera and Frida Kahlo are shared in small boxes throughout the book. Their stories heat my face as I see pain in Frida's paintings and an unabashed drive for a woman's body in Diego's portraits. I feel a little sick. Each one seems to show desire for something not available. Relationships, power, control. I start to question if all of us were never enough for Max.

I spend the rest of the night on TikTok in the dark. I move past a video of Luca doing tricks and moves. His smile is so warm; I can see why people think he's an angel. Sometimes I even want to believe he is. It'd be easier. There's one video of him volunteering at an inner-city middle school where other Latin American kids are doing a series of tricks after him.

I move on to other videos from Native creators. I usually watch Native TikTok where a bunch of people from different tribes explain why they braid their hair a certain way, why they dance, creation stories. And others make funny videos of inside jokes about aunties at powwows. I come across Nicole's sister, who has gone viral a few times with her designs. Anthropologie copied one of her sets of earrings, and people got super upset and bought up her entire shop within minutes. Now her shop always says sold out, and her earrings sales are done within an hour. I really love the language videos, too, or storytelling ones. I wish I had a Bribri community here, in my real life. Like Nicole said about her old boyfriend. Someone who understands, whom I can try to understand back.

I don't get my assignments done. I don't even care. I haven't wanted to go to class for the last couple of days. I thought Grandpa's being here would change things for me, because it was magical the day he got here, but by the end of the day, everything is heavy and dim again.

7-ELEVEN GAS STATION

School doesn't greet me well. I get a few new written warnings from some of my teachers again, and I throw them away so Mom won't see them or maybe so I don't have to see them. I try to avoid Nicole, because even if I'm here, I don't really want to talk to anyone.

After school, I go to work. Hardly anyone comes into the station, so I watch a video of a woman reporting from a costume fair at an orchard nearby. It's funny because the shot was live, and a child dressed as a cow comes skipping through and runs into the cameraman. The video shakes, and the reporter asks if the child is okay. The child runs off, and then the reporter laughs awkwardly and turns back to the camera.

"Well, we're sure having fun today," she says. The video ends.

I replay it a few times just to laugh. Then I read the paper. I get bored and pull out my phone again. The door dings, but I don't look up. I watch the stupid video again. It reminds me of the picture we have at the house on a shelf—Dad dressed infant me up as a chicken, stuck a red cleaning glove on top of my head, and sat me up on the couch to watch TV with him. Mom took the photo while she was pregnant with Max. The photo doesn't feel dishonest. It's real. It's the closest thing I have to Dad loving me. Sometimes, when no one is looking, I settle my head right in front of that grimy silver frame on our shelf.

A customer dings the bell on the counter, and I look up from my phone. It's Luca. And he's got three energy bars and a bottle of water in his hands. I freeze.

He tosses the items onto the counter without looking me in the eyes. "Ring me up."

I can see my hands shaking as I stick one out from under the Plexiglas to grab the bars, and I am grateful for this clear wall between us. For once, maybe the cage goes both ways.

"What the hell is wrong with your hands?" Luca asks. "You scared of me?"

I shake my head.

"You're the one who screwed up my senior year."

"I don't know what you mean," I manage to say while I take the bottled water and start scanning, but it's difficult because of the shaking.

"You're going to act like you didn't have something to do with Nicole breaking up with me?"

"Nicole made her own decisions." I scan the water. Heat in my chest returns as I remember what he said to her. Cool, Jay. Stay cool. "But I do see through you," I add. "You don't think that I can't see you're an asshole?" I say while I press Enter to get the charge.

When I look up, his eyes are flashing. Arms bulging and hands wringing. And I do, I feel afraid. I don't want to fight. My upper arms are quivering now. "Shut up," he says like a threat.

I look at him and remember what I have the right to do if I am ever threatened. There's a sign with instructions behind the counter. I swallow.

"Get out of the store," I say.

"What?"

"Get out of the damn store," I say. Luca ignites and slams his hand on the Plexiglas where my face is.

"Why don't you come out here and make me?"

"No."

"I need that water. I just ran like hell out there."

"You can get free water over there with the cups before you leave."

His face twists, and he leans in and pounds the Plexiglas with both of his arms. Hard, the clear wall reverberates. I feel like wax.

"Fuck you, Jay." His eyes harden at me. He knocks over the penholder, and the pennies in the attached tray fly over the floor.

I watch him walk away. His shoulders squared. I am shaking so hard I have to lean myself on the counter. I breathe slowly and try to take control. I rub my forehead and look at the pennies on the floor. What a damn mess.

BED DAY I

Max leaves at five thirty a.m. to go to school and paint, and I wake up early and ask if I could drive him, save him some time. But he shakes his head. He says that he has to get his application in this week, no time to eat, and that his walk is part of his preparing process.

Maybe it's that I don't want to go to school alone. Or maybe it's that I wish I could whisk myself away into something, like he does with art.

Either way, I'm scared of facing Luca. My shaking comes back when I think of going to school alone. I go back to bed and tell Mom I am not feeling well, and she lets me stay home. She calls Ms. Hannan to tell her I won't be there for our meeting.

Mom stops by a few hours in. *Jay? You okay?* I tell her I'll be okay soon, even if I don't know I will. I do not know what to do. In fact, I have no desire to do anything. Grandpa drops off a few books. A poetry collection. One of ethnomathematics he bought for me. I am too tired to look.

I call in sick to work and have nowhere to be. I doubt that Max would even notice me missing from school. I get a text from Nicole, but I'm not responding to anything today. No, I don't want to go to class. No, I don't want to see Luca again, because I don't understand how to make this any better.

BED DAY II

I don't tell Mom when she asks, but I think it is partly sorrow here with me. It lies in my limbs, in my chest, even in the ache of my shoulders from spending the day hardly moving. And it holds me and tells me *it* needs the comfort of my bed, *it* needs solitude. I sleep on and off; I pray on and off. I know God isn't one to make things easy because I pray. But God, at least, is good at listening.

I tell God I feel lonely and how I miss my brother. That I want my mother back. That I hope I didn't make things worse for Nicole. I ask him if there is anything he could do. *That* prayer is familiar. I ask if he knows if Dad could change and also that I don't want Dad to come back. I ask him why this sorrow I have feels so comfortable and needed when Max is in the world doing so well.

There's a knock on the door, and I look at my clock. It's almost four p.m. My voice cracks when I say *come in*. It's Grandpa, carrying a ceramic plate of sourdough toast. He offers it to me, and I slowly move to sit up and say, "Thanks." Grandpa's face is soft, and his thick dark eyebrows pull together slightly as he looks at me.

"Can I sit, dawö'chke?"

I nod. He sits there for maybe a half hour looking over a book.

He pats my leg. "I love you, dawö'chke." I don't respond, because it's so hard to talk, but I know that I love him. He smiles like he knows and goes back to reading. The rustle of his page-turning helps me to fall back asleep, the warmth of another body in the room is comforting, and for the hour he is there, I feel a little less alone.

NEXT MORNING

I wake up to Grandpa and Mom talking downstairs in hushed voices. I smell sweet hot chocolate, and it must wake the ancestors in my body, because right here it's like all my people who came before me are pulling at my bones. They give me a push upward. And they are successful—together, we take some ground. I shift my legs to the side of the bed, pull on sweatpants and a white T-shirt. Grandpa's low words are enough to get me to the hallway. I take slow steps to ease over the creaky wooden panels. I want to hear what he is saying uninterrupted. But my people always know when you're coming. Grandpa still has all his rain forest sense—the kind that can hear if a snake will fall from the roof of a rain forest before it does.

At the top of the stairs, I look down into the kitchen and see Mom in her pajamas, sitting with Grandpa. They talk over plates of rice, beans, yuca. Their hot chocolate in hand. I hear hints of Grandpa's wisdom; I hear words like *rest*, *heal*, with whispers of repeated *patience*. Our people don't speak loudly, because in the rain forest, even a whisper can be too much noise. Grandpa told me once that when he moved here, his voice grew hoarse from being expected to always talk over something—other people, the cars, the planes. But here, he doesn't have to. They talk quietly, and my ears are not yet used to it.

After a moment, Grandpa stops and turns to look at me on the stairs.

"Míshka, Jay. Ìs be' shkẽna?" he says.

I take a step down and say, "Bua'ë. Bua'ë. Mom?"

"Bua'ë. Bua'ë, Jay," Mom says. "Bua'ë. Bua'ë."

She motions at me to come to her. When I do, she leans in to give me a hug. "I'm glad you are up. Hungry?" I shake my head. She takes a lock of my hair and says, "Mijo, your hair is getting so long."

"Nothing like Grandpa's," I say.

"Time, time," Grandpa says as he takes a sip from his mug. Then he looks at the clock. "Maybe take your tsuru to-go, dawö'chke?" He eyes the rambler by the pot.

"Wëste wëste," I say. I don't take my backpack, because I know I can't go upstairs again or I'll stay there. I fill the rambler, slip on my slides, zip up a hoodie from the front closet, and snag the keys from the shelf.

"Se ne süwe," they call to me as I'm out the door and down the front steps.

Together, we see. Together, we are—through whatever today brings.

THURSDAY

I decide to sit in the lunchroom because I haven't seen Nicole yet. I sit at the end of one of the tables. I have a spoon in a pudding and then take a bite. I haven't sat in here for a long time, and I realize the buzz of people is actually kind of nice. Friends talking, showing one another something new they're wearing, some even dance a little while playing music from their phones. All against the pasty yellow walls of the lunchroom. In a way, it seems like people have moved on from what happened with Luca and us. Now, I'm sure, everyone knows that Luca and Nicole have broken up and have had a few weeks to make it a new normal and whatever that then means for me. Someone even smiled at me in the hallway outside AP Bio this morning.

"Long time no see," Nicole says. One of the girls she was friends with in middle school is behind her. Amber. They both sit down with me.

"How are you, Jay?" the girl asks.

"Oh . . . fine—"

"Because I heard that someone saw Luca going wild on you," Amber says.

"What?"

"Yeah. Warren Reyes was walking by the gas station, said he saw Luca banging on that glass thing?"

"Plexiglas," Nicole says.

"Right. So is that what happened?" Amber is leaning in over the table. Her brown saucer eyes on me.

"Yeah, I guess. He was pretty upset." I keep my eyes down. I'm not used to people talking to me like this. I take another bite of pudding and then look over at Nicole. "He thinks I broke you two up."

"My God. He needs to get over it," Nicole says, shaking her head.

"So here's what I'm thinking," Amber says, leaning back and folding her hands. "Well, actually, it's sort of Nicole's idea. But we should let everyone see him for who he is."

"Sorry. What?" I ask. I think the last time I spoke to Amber was in the third grade. I don't see how people can just avoid me and then want to somehow help me overnight.

Amber rolls her eyes and enters a speech on never liking Luca. "I just think that people need to be called out. To me, it doesn't seem like he's changed or grown. I mean, he came and threatened you, Jay?"

Nicole looks away at Amber's last point.

"Okay, but how would we even do that?" I ask, and laugh. "Luca is a master at getting people to trust him." Even his argument with Nicole at the theater, it was off to the side. No one would have caught it unless they were looking.

Nicole laughs. "Well, I realized your gas station takes security footage. Already on a file somewhere, I promise you."

I sit back, a little floored, and maybe a little honored. That someone would think this way for me, but this is for both of us, for more than just us. "This is why you're the brilliant one," I say.

Nicole half smiles. Though I think we both feel like if we could avoid this we would. "Thanks."

Amber leans in again. "Nicole's mom has a favor to call in from the owner of the 7-Eleven."

"That is true. Mom refinanced his house and helped him out during the recession. And Shelly knows a decent cause when she sees one. She's never really liked Luca."

"Sounds like Shelly," I say. I think of all the benches with her grinning face on it. How she makes bank, works hard.

"So you sure you're okay with that? If we were to go get this recording?" Nicole asks.

"Sure."

"Heck yes." Amber grins, and maybe I appreciate her and laugh a little.

"I'm just going to say, he's led me on a time or two, and was a jerk to my brother when he didn't make the shot in finals last year."

I hope there aren't others whom Luca's hurt. But if there are, they probably wouldn't mind something like this coming his way, either. At some point, I guess, it's true that we cannot hide ourselves, as much as we might want to. Maybe we are simply just stepping out of the way. I mean, this time Luca was seen, too.

LIVING ROOM BLUES

Grandpa loves Billie Holiday. When I get home, he is playing her record. He sits on the couch and leans back, closing his eyes. I sit with him, for once feeling somewhat at peace.

"If you listen close, you can even hear sadness cracking her voice. But she's singing through it all," Grandpa says. I watch him flinch in anticipation before each painful and beautiful note.

One after another plays. A piano solo starts. "Oh, this one." He reaches for the knob to turn it up. "'My Man,' originally a French song 'Mon Homme,'" he explains. I sit back like he does and let her voice sing over us.

Oh, my man, I love him so . . . I don't know why I should . . .

He beats me, too, what can I do?

I shiver and glance over to Grandpa. He turns an eye to me, and we look at each other for a flash. And I know what he's saying. He knows. Mom must have finally told him.

What can I do?

CHURCH

We haven't gone to church for a while. But when Mom asks us if we can go, I agree, and Grandpa comes along, too. Max is turning in his application today and has been a bucket of nerves and moody whenever I see him.

I see Dad when we walk into the sanctuary. He is in a pew by himself, wearing his work clothes. I swallow, my hands shaking already. Grandpa takes my shoulder as we walk in. It could look like he's steadying himself, but I know he is steadying me.

As I look at Dad, I feel like nothing will change. I am Thomas the Doubter. Not that Dad is Jesus or anything, but more like I need to stick my finger in his side to know if he's transformed. And right now, I would be prone to digging my finger in too deep.

He doesn't look over at us. I'm grateful Max didn't come, because I don't know if he could handle it. But Grandpa, Mom, and me have become our own pew. I take Mom's hand, and she gives it an extra squeeze back.

OLD-MAN MUSCLE

I watch Grandpa work outside after the service. He wanted to chop wood for fires. His back is strong. If I go out, I know he will say he is all done, because he likes to be alone when he does this kind of work. He places each piece of wood vertical, lifts the ax behind him, carries it up and over his head, and lands the ax to split the wood perfectly in half. With a small smile on his face, he creates a tidy pile for the next fire.

To work so beautifully. To execute a simple action, to have it all to yourself. And then, to find a little joy. I am jealous yet again.

BACK

Late at night, I hear a loud bang at the back door. I already know it's him. Mom opens it, like she does. And I hear it, the lick of fist to skin. We are all downstairs in a moment, Max at my heels. I see Dad's hands go hard to her neck. Grandpa throws the phone at me. Max jumps on Dad. I make the call. I make the damned call.

Dad is arrested, and he is so drunk he tells the officer that he has beaten his wife only three times, but "it wasn't that bad."

VIII

MAX

I dream about a yellow slide,
there are smoking women
on dark grass standing by,
like pillars, posts. I slide
down on my
stomach,
and you'd
think my skin
would catch, but
it doesn't. The slide
twists around the tallest hill
of our town, bright
yellow, not dull like
the slides in
the nearby
park. I'd
like to think this
dream means the house
is safe and bright again,
but I am not sure.
In fact, I think
I am
wrong.

If you would stop by
the studio, Jay,
I'd tell you about my
art—how the blue
slide painting,
I sold
nearly
right away
to the visiting
art teacher—
is me hoping for
me and
you.

. . .

I find that I don't
contact Melody to tell her
about Dad's arrest.

She's preparing
to graduate anyway
and go to Michigan.
I got my application in. Portfolio done
before all this.
Ms. Hannan even sent her good word.

When Melody's texts come
in, the days are numb.

She knows what happened.
They all do. Small school.

No one checks on us until all hell breaks,
and then everyone wants to slow the traffic,
get a good look at us, and gawk.

. . .

…

Mom lets us do schoolwork
from home.

She called the principal,
asked for permission, and they
were all understanding.

We didn't know what
would happen. A trial,
a sentence. And it came
quickly.

Pastor talked sense into
Dad, got him to plead
guilty.

I can already hear him,
his messages about healing,
about when you do wrong.
You don't fix a bad situation
by doing worse. You do all you can
to make right. You don't try. You just do.

…

...

When I do read my messages,
I see one from Melody asking,
Would you paint me again?
Maybe here at home?

I yield, *sure.*

I'd met her family,
and they weren't the ones to
say anything. Not to pry.
And really, Melody
and the trees
are my favorite to paint.

...

...
Just after she wakes up,
on Saturday, I meet her in
her kitchen.
...

…
Her family spends the weekend reading books
and watching movies.

Her mother takes photos.
A painting session is welcomed
as an honor and gift.

Her parents chat with me while I set up my easel.
They make me coffee. When her mom gives her a kiss—

she teases Melody because she hasn't
brushed her teeth yet. We all get settled.

I pick my colors and get started.
…

…
She stands.
She slouches
a little.

Her short sleep shorts,
a tank top, sports bra.

Cereal bowl in the back.

I smile, realizing it takes two
to portrait.
…

The canvas takes shapes
well. I give it a lime-green
background—
the color of
the walls.

Her parents
grin at each
other over
coffee mugs.
Lovely, her
mom says.

In goes the sink,
the brown
cabinets. Then the
linoleum floor—
bright yellow.

Wonderful. Her
dad laughs,
sticks his tongue
out at Melody,
who tries not
to smile.

…
Melody's legs are so pale,
her pink-brown freckles on her calves
are faint. Her hair is a tussle
of wild and sleepy here on this
canvas.
…

...
I capture her eased
slouch—what a gift to
slouch, to ease through breakfast
just this way.
...

...
Everything is so normal,
I almost can't bear finishing.
...

...

Afterward, she sits with me
in Mom's car and paints
her toenails on the dashboard
so we can talk without
her parents around.

Windows down, the red
paint drips
on the dash. *Shit,*
she says, and I say
that's the easiest
lie for me. Paint.

She settles the
tiny jar into
one of the drink holders.

So how are you really doing?
she asks, leaning back.
Is it so terrible to be messed up? I ask.

...

…

She reaches out and holds my hand.
I'm sorry about it all.
And I think of what I could have done.
That I should have been the one to call
years ago.

But I don't tell her,
because she has all this hope.
A life that never told her otherwise.
The thought probably never crossed
her mind, that I could be
selfish. I could have been wrong.

She leans over and kisses me.
We kiss hard, and I cry, and
she doesn't say anything about it,
because she's crying, too.
She forgets the nail polish jar
there. I pocket the paint
and drive home.

…

At home, Jay, you are a swift shadow again. One room to the other. One of those surrealist paintings with dark door after dark door. You have quieted into nothing. Sleep, then rise, then work, then sleep, skip school, and, yet, I still cannot get your opinions out of my head even if you have closed the door. Only, I don't seem to ever be able to say anything back while I feel it all.

...
I think you're
avoiding something.
I think you cannot face yourself.
...

…
And, Jay,
I want to try
to face myself.
…

IX

JAY

VISITOR

Grandpa calls up the stairs to me. "Nicole is here for you, Jay."

I turn over in bed.

"Coming." I pull on sweatpants and tug a zip-up hoodie over my T-shirt. The pants sag on my hips, and I can already tell I've lost even more muscle weight.

I come down the stairs, and Nicole puts her backpack down, face stern for a moment, and then gives me a big hug. I think she's crying, because I hear a muffled sound of her trying to say something.

"Are you okay?" she says.

"I probably smell like shit."

"You do." she laughs.

I see Grandpa already heating up some water.

"Tea, Nicole?" he asks.

"Please. Mint if you have it."

We sit down on the couch.

"So when did you find out?" I ask.

"Well, first, Mom, of course. She knows everything that happens here."

"Oh right. And everyone knows already at school?" I ask.

"Of course, some freshman with some parent who's an officer couldn't keep their mouth shut."

"I guess it's fine. Who knows what they'll all think of me now." I laugh.

"If you ever come back." She gives me a shoulder.

"I'll come back. I am just so tired."

"I get it. I do," she says. Is this what friendship, kinship is? Getting each other. Or knowing each other long enough to get each other even if we don't fully get it?

"Come back soon, though, okay?" she adds.

"I will."

Grandpa comes over with two mint teas for us, and we thank him.

"Of course. I'll be in my room if you need anything else," Grandpa says with a smile.

"I've got some schoolwork for you," Nicole says as Grandpa heads upstairs. She pulls a few worksheets from her bag and an assignment that looks like she wrote the prompt out by hand for me. She sorts through papers and pulls out a few more.

Then looks up the stairs to make sure Grandpa is away. "And I have something a little extra." She pulls out a USB and puts it on the table.

"No way," I say.

"Like I said, my mom had a favor."

"Have you watched it yet?"

"No, thought we could watch it together. See what we're working with."

I think about Amber mentioning Luca being a jerk to her brother. And then I have to ask. "Did he ever hurt you, like hurt hurt?"

"He had a way of squeezing my hand really tight when I did something he didn't like. He did that before you guys stepped in. I had honestly been missing Aaron a lot then, and he called me some pretty colorful names for wanting to break it off."

"That's terrible."

"Yeah," she says. "He really was controlling. I can admit that to myself now." I am sick that he'd ever do something like that. My father's words are their own kind of fist. I remember all that Mom has been called, too.

"So this"—she lifts up the USB—"is for all of us," she says.

"I'm all for it."

THE RECORDING

She plugs the USB into her laptop and clicks on the video file. At first, the screen is black with a time stamp in the corner, then it flips to the cashier. It's me silently watching that video on my phone.

"I'm so good at my job." I laugh, and Nicole chokes on her tea. I sit next to her at the kitchen island.

I have my head down as Luca comes in. Though the video doesn't have sound, I know there's a ding that happens at that point. Which I always ignore. Customers don't need me watching them. Luca doesn't see it's me working there yet. He is in a sweatshirt. His cheeks look ruddy, and some of his hair sticks on his forehead from sweat. He browses through the snacks. Grabs two energy bars. Then another. Then he walks to the back, grabs a big water.

Then he looks up and sees me unaware of his presence. He stands up straight, with those piercing eyes. Does he have any other look? And then he walks up to the counter and rings the bell. I see my body go rigid. Frozen. He throws the items onto the counter.

"Jerk," Nicole says under her breath. He says something, but no one can hear it. I don't even remember. But you can tell in the video he is already upset at me.

And you can tell I'm freaked out of my mind. I can see my hands are shivering even in the video. I'm trying to hold them steady, but they are not stopping.

Nicole puts her hand on my shoulder.

My head shakes in the video. Luca is spitting at me while he talks. I am now taking the items from his side of the Plexiglas.

Luca is still angrily talking to me while I start to scan the items.

I can see myself relax for a second; I say something back. Luca's body is getting angrier and angrier. I press a button on the till and look at him.

Luca hands are in fists. Muscles coming through that thermal shirt. He says something.

I seem nervous and look around. That must have been when I saw the sign about my right to kick people out.

I say something.

Luca gets closer to the Plexiglas.

I say something again.

Luca smacks the Plexiglas exactly where my face is. I don't flinch. I'm a little proud of myself for a moment.

It looks like I say something. I remember now.

"I told him he could take some of the free water."

"You did not!" Nicole says.

Then there I am, and Luca takes both his arms and slams them on the Plexiglas. I start to shake again despite the fact that I'm not there anymore.

"Damn," Nicole says.

"Yeah, oh and then he, the last part—"

Luca shoves the penholder, and pennies scatter over the floor.

"Ugh," Nicole says.

Luca storms out the door, and I can see that whatever controlled state I was in falls apart. I am back to shaking in the video. So hard I had to lean over on that counter. And then I even sat down. I don't remember that.

"Damn, I'm so sorry, Jay."

"I'm so sorry, too."

"It was awful," she says. "It's all awful."

This is the first time I've ever *seen* myself. And it was really hard to see what other people might see. The shaking Nicole had seen in me before this. The countless times I've felt this way off camera. I look scared out of my mind. I didn't even know it was this rough. My stomach turns.

SHADOWS

With Dad gone, I thought I'd be released of all my fears, but they come back as memories. They are still here. I have dreams where Dad's hands hit me across the face, harder for calling the authorities on him. I have flashbacks, too, when I do something like take out the trash. I see the time he decked me for not taking it out and how he marched me out to the alley and pushed my face into the can so hard the plastic edge cut into my skin.

But now, the house holds all these moments. The door to Mom's bedroom, the one I've blocked from him. The stairway that he once dragged Max down. The living room where he stopped being so secretive and took to smacking us right in front of Mom, and she couldn't do anything but beg in fear of losing everything. This house. This idea of family.

Max gets home and side-eyes me because he's started to go to school again. He was gone all of last Saturday, too.

"You haven't moved," he says.

I don't answer him. What can I say? I don't know how to get through all this.

SMALL STEPS

Nicole says she'll wait with the video. Give me some time. Grandpa comes into my room when I can't make it to school again. He sits with me in the room, and after an hour or two, he says, "Dawö'chke, be wary of all this sadness. Be wary of all this stuff that brings you no joy. You don't even like video games."

"I know, Grandpa. I'm just tired."

"We are all tired. Sorrow has a way of taking everything else from you. Don't listen to it when it says such things."

I think Grandpa fears for me. "Sadness is not uncommon for our people," he tells me. "We have been hurt by many. People have been murdered. Our lands taken. But, in turn, when you are so hurt, you cannot let them win again by allowing them to take your mind. We've got everything against us, dawö'chke, but we're still here, aren't we? Each one of us made it. And we will still make it through all we're facing."

"How do you make it through?"

"Small steps, Grandson. I used to get sad, too. You know your great-uncle? It was so much he took his own life. I don't want that for you. Here, come outside with me. You can help me garden. Did you notice it's spring now?"

GARDEN

I put down my computer, pull on some clean pants, and follow Grandpa outside to Mom's old potato garden. I see he's made up two new raised beds with beautiful deep wood. He's bought seeds for spinach, leaf lettuce, purple cabbage, and onions. Small envelopes of kale and carrot seeds. He asks me to bring over bags of dirt by the garage to begin filling up the beds. It's rich, dark dirt. Grandpa, I know, if he buys something, he buys it to last. If he buys the earth from someone, he wants to be sure to use it for a long time.

We don't talk, and it's peaceful enough to keep away from my thoughts and move through the motions. I pray when one stray thought busts through. I walk to the garage, and my arms reach farther with ease, and each bag feels like a good weight on my shoulder as I carry it to the raised beds. As I work beside Grandpa, I see how much taller I am than he is. He's just above my shoulder. I've inherited Dad's height, and I guess it brings me peace to think about using it to help Grandpa. If I am tall, I decide, I will use it for my people. As far as Max and I know, we could very well be the tallest Bribris in the Midwest because so few of us leave the territory. But I see that Grandpa has been in the sun, and his skin looks so much more alive than mine. I've been inside, away from the sun, and my skin looks like a tired brown. Almost gray. And part of me is ashamed to have denied my body the sky.

When we finish filling the beds, Grandpa tosses me a dowel and a knee mat, and his knees go straight into the grassy yard. We don't say much, but it's good to get my hands in the dirt and hold the raw land. It is right to have the sun on my back. And I wonder if I should try to come out more often.

X

MAX

. . .

Melody and I sit in the back of Dad's
truck for a long time.

I say no to her when
she asks about sex.

She asks me if I want to.
And I tell her that
want isn't the right way
to put it.

I want to, but
I can't tell her I fear that I'd
hurt her like Dad
hurt Mom. I just
say, *I can't.*

. . .

…

We sit there in the truck
doing nothing and saying
nothing, until she turns and
smiles, kisses my cheek.

I drive us back to school since lunch is
    already over.
I don't paint as much over lunch hour
    as I did
before Dad's arrest. I don't have an ap-
    plication deadline, and I'm growing
    tired.

Instead, Melody and I go out
the back door to her car sometimes,
    and
we drive as far as fifteen minutes will
    take us.

Sometimes it's a budding cornfield,
sometimes it's by the orange-
chipped water tower,
sometimes we get to the river.

We hold hands.
She'll point things out and say,
What if you painted that?

…

…

Sometimes her suggestions bother me.
Grandpa does not attempt to provide inspiration.

He just is. And those who just *are*
are the best of subjects. Melody is like that, too,
but I wonder if I've let her in too close.

I am greedy with my inspiration. It must
come from me, from my own desire to do so.

But I know to hide this from Melody and instead—
Maybe, I answer her. *Could be.*

I have told Grandpa about Melody,
and he tells me to be careful with secrets.

I consider his words at the thought
of the end-of-year prom. And how
I plan to keep it from Jay, too.

…

. . .

I remember, Jay,
when you said
no one *liked* liked *us*—

You and I went to one dance
together our freshman year.

It was a garden party, and
we wore shirts with palm prints
and mangoes, green and lush;
we decided to inhabit the Talamanca
   garden.

I remember you dancing, Jay.
You've always been the better dancer.
I remember you bringing in good
   moves.
Pulling in folks in a curious circle.
And the girls did look. I saw.

. . .

…

We had stayed for only an hour while
    Mom waited in the parking lot.

It was a night to be in another place.
I remember us laughing at the
sex-garden references
in the Bible—
Eden, then the gardens in Song of
    Solomon.

Now, Jay, I just keep thinking
how God didn't want us to be alone.
We need community.
We need each other.

    …

…
Melody wears blue sparkles,
and they flash white. Her theme
under the sea.

It's like she is in the water
and all the glass and gems

from the ocean floor
came up on her.
…

...
Others are watching her,
their flashing, hungry eyes—

I will lay them out.

…
If they touch her,
I will lay them all out.

                    …
                    I tell myself
                    they aren't. I say,
                    It isn't such a big deal.
                    …

…
I wring the pocket
of my cheap dress pants
until they rip.

I look down
at the end of the night
…

                    …
                    I have convinced myself
                    I shouldn't be here.
                    Have I become you?
                    …

...

We walk from the gym.
She stands in front of my
tree painting in the art room.

...

I have her stop and take a picture
with my phone,
in the limey fluorescent light,
and I already plan in my head
how to paint her the
next morning before class.

...

…
Before we get to the hall,
she turns off the lights,
and then I kiss her, and we kiss, and we kiss,
by the dark door.

My hands through her hair,
up the back of her neck.
And we're strong.

We're so strong.
…

...

Are we really that strong?

...

…

That night, when you come home from work at 12:05,
you finally tell me what you've been thinking,
You don't spend time at home anymore.

I already knew you wouldn't go to the dance,
and I realize the possibility likely didn't even
come to your mind. This week, you've
only gone to school twice.

I'm tempted to ask you again,
Why don't you go anywhere?
but this time I decide
I don't care.

…

…
The next day,
I do the laundry.

You drift by me
and ask if I need *you*
to buy more laundry soap.

And for a moment
it sounds like the voice—
and I say it—
You sound like fucking Dad.
…

                                        …
                          You shake your head.
                        Never say that to me.
                        You leave the doorway
                          to the laundry room,
                    I pull out my dress pants
                            from the dryer.

                                        …

...
The pocket has frayed.
I swallow.
...

...

When I get home from painting after school, I find you digging through my dresser.

What are you doing? I ask.

You ignore me. *Stop,* I say, pushing your hands away. You're breathing hard.

Where is my red sweater I used to wear? The one with the band of yellow at the wrist?

Your eyes are sharp.

I don't know, I lie.

I saw that girl Melody from school with the same one at the gas station.

And? What, you need more sweaters? It's the only thing I could think to say.

You stare at me with half the rage you give Dad—the betrayal half.

So that's what you've been doing? you continue. *Is that why you've been gone? Is that where you were when you left Mom alone?*

Shut up, Jay. My body is swelling with heat, and my fists bunch.

Dammit, Max. You don't even fucking care. You don't know what it feels like to have to care. I've had to be the one to keep you and Mom safe. And you get to run off. And you're, you're angry. Busy off in your own fucking world.

At least I'm doing something with my damn life, I yell at you.

And leaving our family behind, you say.

...

206

...
And this time,
I'm not holding back.

I go for you first.

I drop my coat on the floor,

I go for your ankles,

and your back cracks

against the wood.

I pull you through the door,

down the hallway. I

drop your legs and

I'm on you,

swinging and swearing.

I take the dirty shots.

I tell you

        you aren't living.

I tell you

        you're too damn smart.

Too damn

        depressed. You get

a few shots at me,

           but I'm winning.

Until something hits

           me over the head—

           It's *Grandpa.*

           And he has a big book in his hand.

Jay, you take the keys from the kitchen table and leave.

Your bloody

                nose

                        drips pink on the carpet,

                                and I want to die.

What the hell did I just do?

XI

JAY

ENEMIES

Are we no longer Jonathan and David?
I never expected to become Cain and Abel.

DRIVE

I take off my shirt and place it against my throbbing nose. I know I can't walk the neighborhood like this, a bloody brown boy with a dad in prison.

Max yelled that I wasn't living, but here, this pain, this blood is me alive. Me putting this shirt to my face—this is being alive.

I drive a few miles out to some soy fields, pull over, and lean the seat back. The pain gets to me. The fist gets me more. And I'm crying. I lean my face away from the road so no one can see me. I pull my knees to my chest and lie there until the sun finishes going down.

SLEEP

When it's dark enough, I go back into the house. I sleep in the living room. I tell Max in my head over and over again, I am *living*. I'm just having a hard time. I'm messed up, and I've got nothing. Now I have less.

XII
MAX

...

My mind is sore,
a swell of gray twine I've
seen in a fabric sculpture.

Guilt is everywhere. It's in the morning
when I look out at the garden Grandpa
and Jay are tending to. It's on the
couch where Jay is sleeping. In the coffee
mug I fill before leaving early for school.

I decide to finally invite Melody to the house when
everyone is gone: Jay at work, Mom in a meeting.
Grandpa volunteering at the local community college.

...

…

When Melody arrives, she looks around the house,
touches the edges of bookshelves, the kitchen counters,
before she looks out the window to our backyard at the new
garden boxes.

The neighbor's dog is in sight. Melody turns
back to the house, and for a moment it
is as if she's healing the walls,
with each touch—

I want her touch
to do the same to me, to tap
me like a maple.
She laughs at me.
What are you thinking, Max?
…

...
I show her my
bedroom, *it used to be just mine,* I
say when I see her touch
the edge of Jay's
bed frame, but it doesn't matter
because soon we're on
my bed—

...

...

And this time, it's me.
We mess around, pulling clothes;
she's musk, honey, stomach,
ocher colors filling my mind
with every kiss and touch
we unfurl on the bed,
until she's over me.

...

...

To my back is the blanket that Jay
and I would fight over years ago.

He'd left it on my bed when
we got brave enough
to sleep alone.

I stop kissing Melody.

...

…

I pull the blanket off the bed,
ask her to go, and I don't tell her,
but it's too much
to ask of her.

Even I know,
I cannot ask her full person
to try to heal all of me.

…

…
It's okay, Max.
I understand. And she
gets dressed and
kisses my forehead.

…

. . .
And again, it's me.
I lie in bed.
Defeated.

God, I'm even crying.
I can't get Jay's bloodied face
out of my head.

All the damage my hands
have caused, the same ones
over Melody.

God, I feel so guilty.
. . .

...

A few days later Melody and I walk around town.
I follow the curve of the cul-de-sac where her house is.

I stop. And then I tell Melody her trailer home is ugly.
She tells me to paint it then. I tell her I mean it.

You don't mean it, she says.
...

...

After the next day
and the next and the next,
I say enough to make Melody
say, *Enough, Max. I've had enough.*
You can't talk to me that way.
She's right. I tell her *I'm not ready for all this.*

She says that she agrees.
It's all over in one moment.

I go to bed early so
I don't have to see Jay.

And really,
I have never felt this alone.

...

...

Mom has picked up after-school tutoring
and restarted her consulting from home.
I had forgotten her handwriting.

At home, I see her charts.
Her pen makes gentle loops like sunsets and eggs.
She is calm with her corrections, still.

...

…

At night, I think about those houses
in Melody's neighborhood.

Those land-ridden trailers.
How they are beautiful.

I think how much I'd give to live so happily
with a family like hers.

She calls to let me know that
if I ever want to connect again,
she's around because she still
cares; she leaves it all in a voice mail.

Then she adds that
she maybe can get why
it all was so hard.

…

...
I find myself with the time I kept for Melody,
and it makes me think of her. I commit to painting again.
I try by the river first.

My body is tired, but I notice the paint's
generosity. Its willingness to spread
itself when I ask.

I paint lines open and expansive
while I think about Jay and me
as kids. How easy it was to run around
the spread of the earth.

How we could lie on the fields with our arms out.
How we grew taller and how it felt right to stretch
for a jar of peanut butter I could never reach before.

I think about braiding Mom's hair,
three lines, woven into one another.
How Jay's hair is getting so long.
Maybe he has been growing in his own way.
...

...

I look at my brown-tipped brush,
place it on the canvas, and

I   pull   the   paint   as   far   as   it   will   go.

Is this us? Pushed to the edge?
Grown beyond what we thought?

...

...

When I come home,
I find Melody's red nail polish stashed away on my desk,
and I can't help feeling that hollowness in my stomach
again. My only comfort—a prayer, another painting.

...

I listen to her voice mail over and over again,
saying that maybe she got why it was hard.
I text her *thank you*;
and maybe she's the first person
I say *I'm sorry* to.
I'm sorry for saying all that about your home.

...

...

I haven't been to the cities in years;
I take Dad's truck and drive two and a half hours
to Minneapolis College of Art and Design—

The school I dream to go to.
The one I've done my best work for.
Ms. Hannan, she's been
helping me to know what to say in my application.
She's written a recommendation letter
and everything after I wrote my own letter to Luca,
not apologizing—I would never do that—
but recognizing that we all could have been
better people. It is sealed in her file,
and I had negotiated to let her send it at
the end of the year. For her, this,
my meetings with her—enough.

Now I am waiting if MCAD will decide I'm
good enough in two ways.

...

...

My heart races as the streetlights flicker
    by.
It's dark, and they all have a glow
—yellow or white.

The buildings of the city are lit,
each a small light, the heat of a
    moment,
a second abode of humanity
and action.

There's a gallery I looked up
that opened today.
I go.
    ...

There are seven
paintings and
four wide walls

They are all of
people in different
positions.

There is no
question in
the room.

In fact, there is
no one else in the room,
just me and these pieces

—whispering
for me to wrap
myself in

                              both—reality
                              and pain,
                              to let it speak
                              to me. Let it
                              heal me,

me—this worthy
tough worship of
image bearing.
…

XIII
JAY

AT SCHOOL

I make it back to school late in the week, a darkened right eye from Max's fist. I try to cover it up with Mom's makeup. I wonder if he is also covering his bruised fists like I had. But most must think it's from Dad because some people still come and talk to me and ask how I'm doing. Some even say *sorry for not reaching out*. My old calculus group invites me to an AP study session, and I go during a study hall. I even crack a few jokes, but I feel empty.

Luca walks into the library. He sees me and storms out.

SNAPCHAT

Nicole calls me while I'm in the library with my group. I step out to the hall to take it.

"Hey, giving you a heads-up, Amber posted the video on her Snapchat story, so people are seeing it now."

"Oh, gotcha."

"Are you okay? I didn't know she was going to post it already. I sent it to her because everyone and their mother follows Amber, and she kept begging me. But anyway. She must not have wanted to wait anymore."

"No, it's all good. I'm not mad. It hasn't really been on my mind much, but I'm glad, I guess?"

"Yeah. But I wanted to tell you in case people start checking on you, you know?"

"For sure. I'll be fine. Hope you're doing okay?"

"Oh, I'm fine." I can hear her smiling over the line.

SPREAD

The video spreads quickly. When I come back to the library, I can see my whole math group has their phones out, showing it to one another. From afar, I wonder if their intrigue is the sweetheart of the school failing or my weakness. I know he's probably never been a jerk to them, and maybe they are doing their own calculations. What goes where, where things belong, where they don't. The imbalance of an equation. And here, maybe Luca is in the wrong. And here, here is maybe me and Nicole getting things right.

But when I get closer, the air is not what I thought it would be. It's not intrigue or surprise.

Derek, whom I used to be closer to, looks at me. "Hey. I'm sorry, man. This is so ugly. Gosh, I'm sorry." His eyes keep blinking, like, I don't know, like how I saw him after his dog died in the sixth grade. I bite my lip.

They all look at me, and they aren't looking at this like a new piece of gossip. No, they are here alongside me. My neck feels hot. I take a breath, and I sit down.

"This is horrible," Katie says. "Was that what happened in the woods?" another one adds.

"You don't have to answer that," Derek says kindly.

I see a few others in the library look at me. Maybe they've forgiven me or forgotten some of the past. Or maybe it's not even about sorting all that out. They know my story. They know about my dad. They can see me shaking. All of it.

I have to step away and head to the bathroom. I sit in a stall and cry.

STUDIO

Max prepares a makeshift studio in the garage so he can keep painting through the summer. Even though I know it'll hurt, I want to talk to him enough that I decide to take a small step, as Grandpa said. I open the door from the house, and the garage is all dark except for one work light. I hear Max before I see him. A stifled sob, heavy breathing. I pass by other easels until I find him bent over on a small red chair, leaning over his arm, in his hand a dipped paintbrush. His phone off to the side.

Now I am able to see his painting. It's good. It looks somewhat like a Picasso, but with Max's twist. Body parts moved around. It is so many people: a girl who looks like Melody, but also a boy-man; they collide with each other.

Then I see my nose.

Lots of red.

I squat down to Max's level and look at him.

"You okay?" I ask.

"Yeah," he says. "I'm trying to get ready in case they let me in." He rubs his nose. "I can't be some embarrassment."

"Want me to stay?" I ask, hearing Grandpa's voice in my mouth, before I even reach for his shoulder.

He flinches.

"No, just go, please."

"Okay." I get up and head back to the door.

"It's really good," I say honestly. "Really good."

PAINTING

The painting stays with me all night as Max sleeps with his back to me. I was wrong for getting so upset at Max. Really, when I saw Melody at the gas station, I wasn't upset at her. She seemed kind. I wasn't angry at Max, maybe I was a little. Hurt.

Grandpa told me after dinner that maybe I should give Max some space and that he and Melody had broken up. In the moonlight, I notice how his hair is getting longer, and it is almost purple—the way our Bribri hair does. I wonder if Melody ever noticed that Max's hair does this in the dark. I hope she did. So many people miss the depth of brownness in our black hair. They forget the earth we need so badly is almost every shade of brown. And blackness is the entirety of the color spectrum, a raven to the sun.

Max's painting is not a raven to the sun, though. It is harsh and bloody. And it scared me with one look. Like I saw all we've gone through in one image. It's hard to see your own violence. And then I wonder if Max sleeps this way, his back to me, so that he doesn't have to look at me. I still have my faint black eye. Maybe home is too painful for Max. Maybe this girl, this painting, have been his peace. For a moment I am glad for him. I am.

MELODY

Max is gone the next day after school when there's a knock at the door, and I open it to see Melody standing there on the front steps. I'm in a small state of wonder at her bravery. I don't know what Max told her about us before everything went down, but I knew she had to be good at keeping a secret because I didn't know about the two of them. And when she saw me at the gas station, I could tell by the way her eyes widened that she knew she was wearing the wrong thing at the wrong place at the wrong time. But now she's got my sweater folded under her arm and a half-filled plastic bag in her other hand.

"Jay," she says. It's a warm voice. "It's good to see you."

"How are you?"

"Doing fine. I kind of hoped it'd be you answering the door," she says. "I've got some things that Max left over at my house, and I figured he'd want them back. You can tell him I'm keeping the paintings. I still really like them, and my parents do, too. I also have your sweater to give back. Which I guessed was yours anyway. Max never wore Adidas or bright red." She hands me the sweater.

"Thanks," I say. "I hope I didn't cause anything between the two of you."

"No, no. I like Max, I do. But he's got a lot going on."

"I think we're trying to find normal."

"I understand. You doing okay? I haven't seen you much at school."

"Yeah. I'm doing okay."

"That's good. I better go," she says, and hands the plastic bag to me. "Also, kind of a shitty thing for Luca to do to you. Makes me wonder about Nicole. I hope she's okay, too."

"Yeah. She's doing fine."

"I'm glad you have each other. I've always wanted cousins like that." She smiles and waves with an awkwardness that she doesn't seem to care about before heading down the front stairs.

SWEATER

Once she's back down to the sidewalk, I close the door and pull on my sweater right away. It smells like laundry soap. When I look in the bag that she brought, I see an assortment of T-shirts and a charcoal flannel that Max must have lent to her. I take it up to our room and put it next to the foot of his bed so that he doesn't think I'm flaunting it.

I head back downstairs and look out the window to the slowly growing garden. I'm proud of it, of the dirt under my fingernails. Dirt. I had been out there all morning when I felt like playing video games again, and it helped. I think about Grandpa's father and mother, who were farmers in Talamanca. *They grew bananas, corn. And roots you'd never find here*, Grandpa told me. Maybe bell peppers and green beans would be something of a wonder to us, too.

MEALS

The garden is bearing like wild. Grandpa and I put the produce in leftover paper bags over the weekend. He shows me how to pickle the cucumbers. We put on his records for the day, and everything tastes like salt, sweat, and dill. Mom makes so many kinds of veggie stews and quiches to freeze, and my body feels better than it had with the frozen pizzas I'd eat every day when I couldn't get myself to school. I've even taken to eating whole green peppers like an apple.

Max stays in the garage all day and comes out only to grab a plate of whatever Mom makes. I don't blame him.

After dinner, I read a book Grandpa bought for me, a whole college textbook on ethnomathematics around the world. The food, the quiet company, I feel like I'm living again.

LATE APRIL

NICOLE: Turtle Lake after school?

JAY: Down.

TURTLE LAKE IN SPRINGTIME

Buds are bursting into flowers. A few apple blossom trees are along the pathways. I arrive, and Nicole is leaning on a trunk looking out at the lake. She's got a black hat and must have trimmed her hair recently.

"I could about kill Amber," she says, smirking at me.

"Nah. It was all good. I didn't mind. Had to happen sometime." I start down the path, and she turns to come along.

"Apparently, Luca's finishing the semester online," she says.

"Dang. That makes sense." No one had seen him since he left school early that day. The last time I saw him, he was storming out of the library.

"Yeah. I'm not sure how this all looks to his college coaches. But it can't be good."

"I ruined his senior year."

"He ruined his senior year. And he has to deal with that now."

I look at her. She has her face to the sun. Soaking it up. This early spring has meant a lot of rainy days but also sunlight.

"I'm actually feeling good," I say.

"That's good." She smiles. "Me too." We walk on, and the slim squirrels are running across the path. Small brown sparrows are out.

"Was it hard having all these parts of your life shared with the whole world?" she asks.

"I thought it would be terrible if people knew everything about me. But some people really seemed to care and were sorry it happened."

"And that's meaningful for you?"

"It is. People really thought we were monsters. And I guess I appreciate that I don't really have anything to hide. It's all out there, and people can decide if they want to care. And some people do, and that's, yeah, that's something I haven't had. But more so, maybe it's that I haven't had this for a while because the only other person who knew was Max, and he doesn't want anything to do with me right now."

COUNSELING

Ms. Hannan is waiting for me when I walk in and put my backpack down. She has made herself a cup of tea.

"Quite the last few weeks?" she asks.

"Yeah. Well, you know the stuff with Luca, I guess."

"Well, yes, in that we won't be doing any more meetings with him. But I wonder about you, Jay. Luca is Luca. What about you? What do you want to talk about today?"

I think about what this time might look like if it was only for me. Luca gone now. Max in his own sessions.

I think about how I haven't really talked to anyone about Dad. People know, but I guess they really don't *know*. How, if I were to be selfish with this time, to think of my own stuff, that's what I'd like to talk about.

"I guess I'd like to talk about my dad." My hand shakes a little at that word.

"What do you think about that?"

"I probably have some PTSD or shit."

"Could very well be," she says.

"Nicole said you'd try to talk to me like in *Good Will Hunting*."

She laughs. Her tea steaming around her chin before she takes a sip.

"It's not your fault. It's not your fault," I joke. She smiles and takes another sip of tea before leaning forward to look at me.

"Well, you know it isn't, Jay. You have to know that what happened to you is most certainly not your fault. You do a lot to try to save others. To fix others. And when something goes wrong, my guess is that it eats you up inside. So, no, Jay. It's not your fault that you've been hurt. I don't know much, but what I have heard makes me think you've probably endured unimaginable pain, and you've been so strong. It's okay to be the one who needs help, Jay."

I look down because my chest feels opened by her words. A crack in a rock, a waterfall.

XIV

MAX

...
All my thoughts
have turned to painting, art.

And I tell them
yes, yes, yes.
...

…

With every painting,
I learn
        two skin tones,

one light,   one dark,

                      gives muscles to body (definition?)

…

————————————————————

…

…
I have two dimensions of
me|me

from two different times,
present at the same time.

Each project,
becomes
its own.
…

Canvas 4. Portrait. Desired Figuration. Unexpected Solutions.

On Tuesday I see   myself as if I could

only be new   solutions drift

to my face,   whole without

Jay; I hadn't   needed anyone

else there you see I   am often grounded

by others and   it's hardly true joy

to have   others

say   you.

are   you.

and   you.

when   I can

not   say

me me me me me me me me me me me me me me me me me me

max max max

max max max max max

max max max max max

max max max max

max max max

max max max max max max

max max max max max max max max max

max max max max max max max max max

max max max max max max max max max

max max max max max max max max max

max max max max max max max max max

max max max max max max max max Max

The garage becomes my woodshop, too. I take the scraps from the woodshed, find all of Dad's old bent nails from roofing; he'd placed them in a jar, afterward convinced he'd melt them down someday. A new canvas comes in the mail, a gift from my teacher. He heard about Dad. I'd find new materials placed in a cubby or a stack of canvases, white, pre-stretched canvas in the studio. It's kind, but if I don't like something, I paint over it. I try to build the soft thin roofs over my wood blocks, I do, I can't help but feel like Dad when I watched him do this move, so perfect and on target. I take a hammer, whack an uneven nail in behind, looking like broken legs from the back. They hold the canvas together, and for now, it's all I need.

Personality Exploration: Color Palette

Mars   Max Cadmium   Cyan
Black   Orange Blue

Yellow   Warm   Raw
Ocher   Gray   Umber

Burnt   Quina-   Cobalt
Dioxazine   Cridone   Nicole

Blue Joy   Somber   Jay
Liquid Red   Heat   Melody
Bluejay   another   Blue Jay

Sculpture—Talamanca Eagle Before Disarray

In black plastic, red spray,
an eagle above   no savior?
   angry at the men below   up
      eagle demon   up
         descends   up
            snaps him

Constellation Installation

Are   the   constellations   just   various
women   men   children   people
pulled   into   the   sky   and left?
          I   paint   the   stars.
For   Valle   de   la   Estrella,
          each   one,   I   think
of   pieces   of   what   would   have been
     light stuck there.   Reminders to us to keep
shining   the   light.   The   pieces of   God
he'd   place   in   us.

Eagle Figuration

I paint eagles and

vultures and men, wild and angered,

then I paint fighters.

I paint them

crimson mars black horror and evil beauty/grace it feels like

choking to me/to get it out,

like I'm coughing these from me. We must fight the evil inside us,

too.

As it wants to

fight flesh

and

blood, but

no longer.

Jay, you and I,

we must stop

here.

…

You've gained so much depth,
my art teacher tells me when I bring him my best.
You're getting ready to soar.
When he stops by my easel at school
to hand back my sketch ideas
I asked for his thoughts on.

…

Along with a flyer in his hand.
Internship applications.
Maybe
you'll find something here.
A couple summer opportunities
before you start.
A showroom.
He is confident in me;
my throat tightens.

…

...

I do three trash paintings
on my best canvases. I am
scared of slipping backward without
an art school application in front of me.

On the fourth,
I'm sweating as if I am
fighting for this painting.

What is a painting
if not for healing? What is art
if not for transformation?

I have so many angry
paintings, my recollection
of each bruise on my body, on
my own mother's, on my brother's—

Each line I pull is raging and sure,
flung across the canvas.
The drips of red
blood, or nail polish.

...

. . .
I sit, and

for a moment,
I'm back in church,

and this stuck feeling
has me wanting to pray.

I lie down on the concrete studio floor.

Paint in my hair,
my face,

and for a moment,
I don't think about all this,
and for the first time
in a long time—

I think about how maybe
I wish I could talk to Jay.
God, help me.
. . .

XV

JAY

PAINTING OF GRANDPA

Another night when I cannot sleep and my mind is all bad memories, I go out into the garage where Max's home studio and woodworking shop is getting even more scattered. Dried paint dishes, various self-portraits, sculptures even now, half morphed.

Then I see a painting of Grandpa. And it saddens me for a moment. Since Grandpa had been ignored by Max while I was home. Max didn't seem to need him, didn't seem to need any of us. Except seeing Grandpa sitting on that cube, knees out, one arm pressed on his thigh as he looks out at something, the stacks of Max's own paintings in the back . . . I don't know. It is beautiful.

UP NORTH

Grandpa invites me to come up with him to his cabin and help him move back in, un-winter his home. I never want him to leave. He seems to know it's his time, though, and I will never decline the chance to go to Grandpa's house.

We pack up his things and leave. With each mile closer to Lake Superior, the biggest lake in the world and the center of the Anishinaabe universe, the air gets colder and colder, making me all the more aware of my own heat. I leave the window down, welcoming the cliffs, the trees, the woods, the lakes and caverns.

FIRST TASK

First, we warm the house, and then we pull off the panels nailed to the windows that protected them in the cold. We have hammers, and we tug to undress this house.

I feel like this house.

Boxed up for a season of survival. I have survived well like this house. My muscles are as strong as ever as I tear off each panel. It's a good strength, one I don't need to use to hurt. A useful strength, and it has me crying. I start tearing off the wood faster and faster because I can't help but think of each of these boards as a thick skin I had put up. I don't even know what's inside there.

EAGLES

I spot eagles circling nearby. They are beautiful; and I think of the terror, the two men. Here, there is no fear, and if there is, it's because these eagles know to leave us Bribris alone now. An agreement between their larger and our braver ancestors. An agreement, I realize, must always be made in new ways, with new eagles, and new terrors. I am grateful to be like one of the men after the battle. I, too, will take up my basket and head home along the river.

WALK

Today my church is the backwoods of Grandpa's cabin. I'm a few minutes ahead of the sunrise, and I feel like God wants me to be there for this day's genesis. Can I feel this way anywhere else? Perhaps this is like Max's canvas, when he begins something new. Here, with the pines towering over with their plum-rimmed shadows holding me inside them. I watch the young sky redden through the trees' needles as I continue to walk farther and farther out. My body senses range—warmth, coolness.

Before I am set to leave, Grandpa goes into his garage and brings out a wooden desk. He pushes sawdust off it. It's simple, long, but clearly a piece of oak he's saved.

"You were gone awfully long this morning," he says with a wink. "This one's for you."

RETURN

When I come home, no one is there. Max must be in his studio. Mom at a church group. But I see that Max has put my bed back in my old room. And on my bed is the painting of Grandpa. It is laid on my newly made bed with the blanket we used to share folded at the foot. I close the door, sit with my face in my hands, and breathe.

MINNEAPOLIS

Nicole invites me to go with her the next Saturday to Minneapolis to get pizza with her high school friends.

"Are these the ones who thought I was hot?" I ask.

"Maybe," she says, and shrugs her shoulders like she's not telling me anything more.

We take her mom's SUV, and we head to Lake Street. It's alive with murals, mercados, streamers welcoming people into bakeries, so many languages painted on glass. It makes me wonder about Costa Rica, what it might look like in the city. I wonder if it has colors like this? So many people here look like family. It's beautiful.

Nicole laughs at me. "We need to get you out more."

"I forget we're not alone."

"I know. I forget, too. You should come with me to Red Lake sometime."

She pulls into a place called The Bad Waitress, and there's a group of people waiting there who all see her right away and give her a big, big hug. She introduces them, and they're all so beautiful, too. Dyed hair, nose piercings, tattoos. A few of the girls raise their eyebrows at me and at Nicole, and I don't know what to do and realize I am rubbing my arm. We all sit down and order the biggest plate of nachos I've seen. One of her friends keeps checking her phone.

They tell us about their junior and senior years. They update Nicole on the gossip. And I realize that maybe this is what Max and I were, too. Just smutty stuff you say at the end of the year. Stuff you'll only remember for a while and then forget. Nicole is glowing. These are her friends, and I can tell they love her. And then I see Nicole square her shoulders toward the front door. I turn around and see Aaron, the boyfriend in her Instagram photos, come in.

One of her friends who was checking her phone is whispering, don't hate me, Nicole. Don't hate me. Aaron walks over. His body is soft, and his hair is in two braids, and he's wearing a baseball cap.

I look back at Nicole, and she's smiling. I'd say maybe like a fool, but who am I to say that? Maybe this is how Grandpa looked at Grandma years ago. Maybe this is how Max looked at Melody. Before Aaron can say anything, they hug each other, and hug and hug. She kisses him on the cheek. He kisses her back, and then they start really kissing.

It's like we're all at a game or something as we clap and cheer loudly. "Whoo!"

Probably looking like the most annoying group of teenagers. But dammit, I think we're all just happy.

SACRED SPACE

I hang that painting of Grandpa on the wall to the left of my desk. I even got some grasses from the garden and placed them in a jar of water. I put a huge mug I threw in a middle school pottery class on my desk and place pens in it. Mostly pens, a few mechanical pencils. My graphing calculator. The desk Grandpa gave me is larger than most desks you'd see at school.

"You've got too long of legs to fit in some small desk," Grandpa said.

I wouldn't say it out loud, but the grains of the wood are my favorite. Dark and heavy. Strong, like it's not going anywhere. I sit there for an hour. I don't even have anything to do, but it already feels right.

CALL WITH GRANDPA FERNANDO

In my room, I lean back in my desk chair. I call him up on my cell phone and kind of laugh thinking about Grandpa still using his landline because it's the only line that works out in the woods. I can already see him on the stool in his kitchen, right by the platform where we eat breakfast. The phone hooked on the wooden log walls.

He answers right away. I call at six thirty so he can still catch some baseball or finish a book he's on.

"'Ìs be' shkẽna, dawö'chke?"

"Bua'ë bua'ë. Ma be'?"

"Bua'ë."

We talk about his day. He likes to tidy things up. Get stuff ready for whatever the next season brings. And he's got a million +. He tells me that on his daily walk he saw a young eagle catch a fish at the creek not far from him. "Made me think of you and Max," he says. "How are you two doing?"

I'm honest. I tell him that Max gave me a painting of him but that Max still doesn't talk to me much and that I can't figure out exactly what to do.

I ask if Max called him, and Grandpa doesn't answer these kinds of questions.

"What do you think you could do?" he asks.

"I know, I know, Grandpa. We're too old to mess around like kids, so it's not like we can start going places together again and everything would be cool."

"Would you talk to him?" Grandpa says.

"I'm not good at talking. Can't I just be nicer? Buy him some paints. I don't even know what paints he likes or anything."

"Is that what Max really wants? Paints?"

"You saw him; he hardly was home when you were there. Since Dad went to prison, I don't know what he wants. What do you think, Grandpa? Maybe he's lonely after Melody."

"Did you meet her?"

"Yeah, she dropped stuff off."

"Think he still likes her?"

"Probably. But I don't think I could ask him about it. He shuts me down unless he wants to talk. And it's a touchy subject because he was keeping it a secret from me. I feel like he didn't think I wanted him to be happy."

"Well, do you?"

"I mean, I was upset that he was lying to me and didn't trust me enough to at least try to be supportive."

"Would you have been?"

"I don't know. I was in a weird space. Probably not, I guess."

"You know, dawö'chke, I miss my older brothers and sisters every day. It's hard being the baby of the family." I think back to the picture Grandpa always showed us. His siblings all lined up. Each one passed now. I remember how he took flights to each of their six funerals. But didn't think about him mourning all alone in the woods. "So you, you are the big brother. You looked out for Max, but sometimes you don't know what is best for him. And you don't always know what he needs, so you love him like he's joining the spirits tomorrow. Doesn't mean the bad memories aren't around. They are part of you both. Something you both carry. You both had to learn how to carry it on your own. And maybe soon you can come together. Don't you think?"

I swallow because this question is too hard to answer. And it's the kind of question, I know, Grandpa doesn't expect me to answer with words.

STUDIO

When I walk into the school studio at lunch, I see Max is wearing a new off-gray sweatshirt, and I smile, remembering Melody's comment. Though the door closes behind me, he acts as if I am not there and keeps painting. Art books are scattered at his feet. The windows are open, and the sun lights up paintings of figures under umbrellas, flowers, men with big mustaches, tall houses with straight windows.

I sit down on a white box, perch up my Adidas slides, white socks to my midcalf, wrap my arm around a leg, trying to let Max know, *I'm not mad at you.*

I look around at all he's done. Canvases are starting to pile up, and they lean in stacks against the wall. He keeps working on a background. Green, boxy, house-like shapes in the back.

"You're doing a lot," I say.

He lifts his shoulders as if this is the only thing he can do. "I'm planning on moving for an internship. Getting to the cities before I start. If I get in." He doesn't invite more conversation. I lean over my legs and watch him. Each move he makes is a pushing, a shaping. He's working on a green grassy hill. Then a yellow slide.

"You ever get upset at Mom or Pastor? Even Grandpa?" Max says as he keeps his eyes on blotting sand into a park.

"Don't know if I'm there yet," I say. I think about how Pastor and Grandpa didn't know what Dad was really doing. And how Mom was so scared to lose so much, though maybe that wasn't a good enough reason. "I guess a little," I add.

"They should have called on him a long time ago. They are all supposed to be keeping us safe. And look how messed up we are."

I flinch, but I know he's right.

"Like, why the hell did I hit you?" he says. "And why did we beat up Luca in January? Why didn't I just calm everything down? Have you hold him down or something?"

"It was probably me swinging first," I say, and laugh for a second. When I think of it, Max wasn't leading the way. He was the one who sat next to Mom after she'd been hit, made sure that Nicole wasn't injured. Sure, he beat up Luca, but I know that he wouldn't have gone so far if it was him alone.

"I wish I could have protected us more," I say. "I could have called way earlier."

"No, Jay, we did what we could."

"I wish I could have done more."

"We're here now," Max says. "And besides. You were the one who did call. That's something."

COLORS

I have known that Max wants to leave. But now I can see it in his art. It's there. City colors I saw with Nicole—piercing blues, steel silver, blacks, streetlight yellows. I have seen seventeen rounds of change in Minnesota—we are good at living in constant change. We are, I suppose, much like the trees. Our bones and flesh change plenty for the weather. But this bold steel is new, and not us by any means. I can already tell that Max and I will probably not see this next round of change together.

The truth is, I am not angry at him. Maybe it was Max's fists against my face, well, not his fists, but his words telling me that he was seeing me giving up. It's as if the only one I could truly trust for the truth—was telling me the truth about myself. To dream a little. To get out. That we're here now after all this we've gone through.

CHOCOLATE

I tease Mom about finding another man when we stay up late talking. She is stirring hot chocolate in a pot—cacao powder, sugar, milk, cayenne powder. We can't help but want something warm, and Bribris are made for chocolate. Grandpa told me that my great-grandfather used to grow so many plants—cacao among them.

"So what are you thinking about doing when Dad gets out?" I ask.

"Oph. That's a hard question, mijo. We're not moving back together, though."

"You think he can change?"

"If people truly want to change," she says, "they can."

"Sounds like you've been talking to Pastor."

"Oh, sometimes."

She pours the thick chocolate into a cup. Only Bribri women can make the hot chocolate. Mom follows our tradition and has not taught me how. I still try to watch closely. Even if I cannot make it, I never want to forget how she can. Chocolate has so many healing properties. If you take cocoa oil and put it on a cut, it seals and heals it so good you won't know it was there. I used to put cacao butter on the bruises I would get from Dad's hand.

Drinking cacao is the same. Heals us inside.

"Do you still love him?" I ask Mom.

"Another hard question." She doesn't answer it but laughs. "When we first met, he was such a cowboy. He'd wear this big belt buckle and that hat. You know the one downstairs?"

Dad was wearing that hat in that photo with me as a baby. The one where he stuck a rubber glove on my head.

Mom looks up like she's thinking back, because she's smiling a little. "I remember him walking right into the bar, and his skin looked so warm in the bar lights, you know, for a white guy. Like he was tanned from being outside so much. And he actually had been working outside a lot. He was cleaning horse stalls out not too far from there. And when we started dating, he took me out on the horses—probably so he could hold me like that. The horses are so much bigger here than in Costa Rica, too. Big enough to hold us both. It all felt so very American and Bribri at the same time."

She stops and looks into her mug. "And now, something took him away from himself," she says. "It's not for us to find what it was."

She lifts the mug to her mouth. Then pauses before taking a sip.

"Jay," she starts, first looking down at her cup, then back up at me. "I am sorry." She wipes away a few fast tears.

I place my mug down, and she gives me a big hug.

"Not much of a mother, am I?"

We stand and hold each other for a long, long time.

"I love you, Mom."

DANCE

I find Bribri songs on YouTube, and I begin to play them while I read Bribri story translations Grandpa had worked on in college. They all are written out in nice, clear paragraphs. I don't read more than one or two, but after I read, I journal about each one. I pay a little more attention to the numeration we use, how we tell stories, what the math is behind our systems. Everything is balanced in Bribri, a mirror, an evenness. I don't understand it all, but the words are echoes of Grandpa's own voice, echoes of words that feel like home, that feel like safety.

I hear *mishka*, the word Grandpa would call to me as a kid. It means *come here, let's go*. I love the way the word sounds. The action of movement with *missssssshhhhhh* and the abrupt stop of *ka*. The word sounds like it wants you to move quickly and quietly but then to arrive, to stop. The word itself wants you to *come righhhhht here* so we can move on.

MCAD

Max gets a letter in the mail from Minneapolis College of Art and Design. He's offered a minority scholarship that covers 75 percent of tuition if he starts in the fall. Mom cooks up Caribbean coconut chicken to celebrate. Shelly and Nicole come over, and Grandpa drives in, too. We all eat together, and I can tell Max is pleased, though he doesn't say it. He sits back in his chair as Mom chatters on about all the great classes it has and reads off a sample list of classes he could take.

"Mijo, look, pottery."

"Yeah, Mama," Max says.

"I love pottery," she says as she touches the photo.

"You're going to kill it over there," Nicole says, looking over the brochure in Mom's hands. "I'll have to come see you when I'm visiting Dad next year."

"Anytime." Max smiles.

I am happy for him, though it hurts to be. I look at the brochure, and the campus looks like something out of a dream. Big murals swirling up and down the walls. The Minneapolis city skyline behind it, lit up. Students holding lattes from a nearby coffee shop. It's near Eat Street, where the entire world is served in foods. But the flash aside, I see all their successful alumni on the front page doing work in NYC, California, and some Native kids doing some really good work. Winning something called the Jerome Fellowship, having big art shows out in NYC. It's inspiring; it is. Max has worked so hard, and I know he deserves it all.

THREE HUNDRED MILES

When everyone leaves and Max is in bed, I take out a topography map of Minnesota. I think about how we're all going to be spread out, Mom and me here. Nicole and Shelly, too. Grandpa up north, and Max going to Minneapolis. I count all the miles between us with a ruler. Each centimeter is twenty-five miles. Three hundred miles in total.

I know that Max isn't selfish. I'm drawing the straw to stay. Mom walks into my room and looks over my shoulder at the map. She traces with her finger over each dot I drew in a rhombus. "Estrella."

I think of Valle de la Estrella, the Valley of the Star that Grandpa told me about. A valley where our people live among our sister tribe, the Cabécar.

"You know, it wouldn't be so bad having a place to yourself, too," she says.

I shrug.

"I saw you got a thirty-one on your ACT. I dreamed of that score. Seems like a gift." She rubs my shoulder.

"I guess."

"You should think about school, too. Max is not the only one." She places her hand on the map and shows what another dot would be in another city of Minnesota. She picks the twin city to Minneapolis. Saint Paul—me.

She says, and kisses my forehead, "Think about it."

SANDHILL CRANES

It's raining, and I offer Max an early drive to school. He agrees, to my surprise, answering my hope. We both get in Dad's truck. Rain spots the windshield and then is smeared clear over and over again.

We don't talk for the first few blocks. The rhythm of the wipers drone.

"What did you do over the weekend?" I ask. I know the school is closed. His weekends are spent in our garage.

"Some homework," he says. "Went to the river to get out of the studio a bit. I heard you talking to Grandpa some nights."

"Yeah. It's kind of nice to get out of my head a little."

"That would be."

I look out for a moment and spot something tall standing in the middle of a field near Turtle Lake.

"Did you see that?" I say as I quickly pull over.

Tall and brown—two huge birds stand out so clearly in the grass fields. A pair. I gently close the truck door, and I can hear their thick cluck warble. Loud like a maraca, but deep, almost otherworldly. Max is behind me, quiet as anything, looking out, too. The birds' movements are graceful. Once they spot us, they take synchronized slow steps and walk together away. We follow them, watching them move their prehistoric and large bird bodies with their red-capped heads. Their eyes are yellow; they move with a head bob, brown bodies that slink, gray necks curve in the same way, a copy of each other. I think they make their echoing noises to look big, but watching them step together makes me smile. I look back at Max behind me, and I realize that right in this field, Max and I, too, are synchronized. The same, same as the birds.

STILLWATER PRISON

I decide to visit Dad for the first time. I drive Mom's car to the prison, a few hours out, and on the freeway, Mom's Gillian Welch CD plays "Look at Miss Ohio":

> She's a running around with her ragtop down.
> She says, I want to do right, but not right now.

The song sticks in my head, and I wonder what Dad I'll meet here. I try to, instead, dwell on the steady oak and spruce passing by. Row by row.

The guards check me for any dangerous items before I can talk to him in the meeting hall. I sit at a table and wait for him to come out. When he walks into the room, I don't even see the blue jumpsuit, because Dad's face says he doesn't know what to do.

We sit, and after a few moments of silence, he starts crying hard. Like really hard. And then he takes a deep breath, and he starts talking as if he didn't just cry.

"How's school?"

"Pretty good. I have some Cs I'm trying to beat."

"You look really strong. You working out?"

"Almost every day."

"Your brother?"

"He got into art school. But you should talk with him." He nods. Rubs the space between his eyes.

He's quiet for a while.

"I should go," I say.

"Sure, sure," he says. "You're a good kid."

"Thanks."

And then I head out. I don't know exactly why I came other than I knew *I had to.* Maybe he needed to cry. Maybe I needed to face him. I cannot look back, cannot look forward; we are where we are.

BIRDS

I see so many crows on the way home. I park the car and start walking around the block to see how many crows are truly gathering. Collections of these black birds move into our neighborhood like Hitchcock's film *The Birds*. A cat prowls around under a tree. The birds get up like a sigh, their wings half-heartedly spread, getting them two or three feet from where they were.

Then I see the flash of a blue jay wing in a tree. I follow it, so bright in all the darkness. I find him perched in a spruce. Blue jays are a mystery. Sometimes they stay in the winter, but when I see one after no sightings, I know warmth is coming back. I used to think of the blue jay as such a villain, but this season, I understand that the sparrow, the crows, and even the blue jays, do what they do to survive. There are no perfectly benevolent birds. And like they have, I've done what I've needed to survive. He's looking at me. Even for that moment, we are exactly as we are meant to be—at peace in a tree and at rest on the sidewalk. Even if no one else notices, I see him, he sees me, steady and strong in a thick body, resting for a moment, and then gone.

Onward.

COLLEGE

Nicole brings over a bag of popcorn and a stack of college guide-books she picked up from the library. We sit on the couch and look them over, writing down the ones that look good. Although every-one else seems to think I'm ready, I keep imagining Grandpa and me traveling to Costa Rica together. He hadn't returned there for years. His last visit was for the death of his last brother. I remember from one of the bird books I'd seen that a type of blue jay lives in Costa Rica as well.

"I think I'm going to wait a year." I close the guidebook in my lap and tap my fingers over the cover.

"Really now?" Nicole looks up at me past her glasses.

"I think I'm going to take a gap year."

"A gap year?"

"A gap year to Costa Rica like all those hippie kids in those teen-ager movies." I grab a handful of popcorn, feeling a grin tugging at my lips.

Nicole covers her mouth. "Oh my god!"

"Actually, though, you're totally going to do that." She starts shuf-fling together the guides. "You could always hit up the University of Minnesota with me. We can start in the same year."

She couldn't be surer of me. I've always felt that way toward her. Didn't realize she felt that way back.

"So are you staying here for your last year?" I toss a piece of pop-corn into my mouth, remembering what she said about visiting Max when she visits her dad.

"After all this?" She laughs. "Yeah. Actually, I came here to get closer to Mom. And we have, and I want to stay. Though I miss my baby sister. She's so cute and growing up." She pulls out her phone and shows me her background. She does look bigger, walking and holding the hand of Nicole's dad.

"So what about Aaron?" I raise my eyebrow.

She laughs, eyes a little brighter. "We're gonna try again."

"Good for you." I throw a kernel at her. "I think you guys are gonna figure it out."

"I know, I know. Shut up."

Graduation is just a few weeks away. I see Max preparing to leave. He's bought a bunch of new clothes. He's agreed to a summer internship and a couple of smaller jobs that get him grounded in the heart of the city before his classes start. He is going to live in the extra room of an art student who already attends MCAD. He'll have to share a bathroom, a kitchen, but I can tell he is thrilled. And for the first time in a while, I am a little thrilled for myself as I think about Costa Rica. About our territory, the museums, the ocean, it being no longer solely in me, but me in it all.

GRADUATION

We graduate from high school, on the "B" roll. The art teacher gives Max an award for his hardworking artistic ethic. I get an extra nod from Grandpa. They all clap for us—Mom, Grandpa, Shelly, and Nicole—and even Ms. Hannan is there.

We'd gone one after another.

Me first, then Max.

Exactly how we came into the world.

GONE

Max packed up a good amount of his room in those clear, cheap bins. I see rows and rows of black jeans and sweatshirts. He's even ordered a winter coat early, and when it comes in the mail, Mom laughs, pulling it out of the plastic packaging. Black, of course.

"You're really thinking ahead, Max," she says. It's June, and everyone is in shorts and tank tops.

In other bins, I see he has all his paints organized and has brushes in another. His easel packs up into a neat wooden square.

Mom is going to drive him. She is so excited, and though I can tell Max is, too, he's trying not to show it. It shows in his stress as he looks at his watch. In a call he makes to the artist he's staying with, asking if two p.m. was still okay to show up, I realize maybe this is Max's moment to have. That I might take it from him, and I tell Mom I'll stay behind. Mom doesn't debate. She knows I need my own time to quietly take this all in. Meanwhile, Mom is leaping around, getting things in the car. She got it washed yesterday, so it even beams an unnatural silver.

And then, Max is gone.

ANOTHER CALL

"What if I can't leave Mom?" I ask Grandpa on the phone.

"I think you know you can."

"Would you go back to Costa Rica with me?" I see us there again in my head. In Talamanca, my first time, along with him. The land of our people, where he grew up as a boy.

"Of course, dawö'chke," Grandpa says. "I would be honored to go with you."

VACUUM APARTMENT

A man from our church talked with me about a data-entry job and an apartment he has over his vacuum-selling business in town. I feel like I should just go ahead and take it. And when I tell Nicole about the apartment, she laughs and says that of course it's a hard apartment to fill—*vacuum sounds all day.*

Mom gets all teary when I show it to her. She's begun to talk to Shelly about moving herself as well. It is true, what Grandpa says, she is growing sturdy like a mountain, remembering who she is. Her brown skin is looking as warm and bold as ever. She has begun to wash her face every morning, oil it with coconut oil, even cook without being as frugal as possible.

"Good for you, Jay," she says.

Knowing this seems to cut another tie. Another piece I knew wasn't for me to carry.

MOVE

Nicole helps me move my things out to the apartment. I can work from home at my new data-entry job, where, to save up for Costa Rica, I document the amounts of grain collected from one of the grain companies in town. Mom calls me often, but during the day, I have podcasts playing. At lunch, I watch cooking videos from other countries. I set up my desk from Grandpa right at the window. Put a chair close to the other window. Sometimes Nicole comes over, and we play chess, or she makes sure I still remember everything from AP Chemistry that she's planning on taking her senior year. Other days, I listen to the entire Bible on tape, *The Iliad*, and I think of epithets for my family. For Max and me, and I think of us as we were, Max and Jay, the saints of the household. Now, I'd be Jay, the data-entry man. Mom, the chocolate woman. Max, the artist. Dad, the we'll-see man. Grandpa, hermit of the Minnesotan woods. Minnesota, the state of cabins, lakes, and hills, and sans serif welcome signs. Nicole, the brilliant. In this moment, the hard and the good all feel at home with me, as they start to pile up in my head like wheat numbers and pounds of grain.

LOWERTOWN ART GALLERY

I get an invite from Max a month after I move in. The invitation is taped on my door. Max hasn't called since he left. His name feels more like a whisper. We'd never been apart like this, and I keep worrying I'll forget his voice since I haven't gotten the nerve to call him, either.

The invite for an art show in Saint Paul is nicely designed. It sounds familiar because I seem to remember his internship was to paint and upkeep galleries or something. It says it's a "soft opening" before the official public opening. I keep looking at the invite throughout a couple of weeks, and when the day comes, I call work and say I'll be stopping early. I pull a nice jacket on and go out to Dad's old truck. I drive in silence, through the stages of dusk, to arrive in the midst of downtown Saint Paul. I park a few blocks away, navigate with my phone to find a cobblestone path with various noisy restaurants and a theater. I find the address, and it takes me below to a white hallway where people are walking around with drinks in block-colored dresses.

I hear some music, but it seems like there are many rooms people are going into. It would have been nice to bring someone else, but I didn't think of it until now.

As I weave through people, I look in one room and then another. And then I see him. He's wearing well-fitting dark jeans and a black tee. A smart blue suit coat over it. He has his arms at his sides, occasionally rubbing his leg as everyone talks. He sips out of a glass of water and laughs and sips again. Max sees me after a few minutes, makes an exit with those he's talking to, and walks over to me. We don't have to say anything. He takes my arm, and I am surprised by his tight grip, and it lasts as if he'd embraced me.

"So you painted something here?" I ask.

He nods. "Yeah. Here, I'll show you. It's kind of just in this room they haven't opened up yet." He starts walking down the hallway away from people. I follow him.

"I had actually been painting the studio walls white for them, so I could make some extra money, but the owner thought maybe I could fill this room since no one paid for it for the next few months."

He stops at a door, fumbles with a key from his pocket, and opens it to a dark room.

"Go ahead," he says, nodding for me to go in.

I step into the dark, and he dims the light slowly on—

It's the field.

Dark green, emerald edges, and each groove, each smudge above—a mustard field yellow.

For all his understated, silent self, the painting is gold.

Our gold.

ACKNOWLEDGMENTS

All those to thank—what a gift to be surrounded by communities of love, support, and brilliance. First, a great thank-you to Ron Koertge for seeing me and seeing this book. To have a mentor get you, I believe, is sometimes all a young writer needs to start this journey.

A thank-you to my dear, long-time writing friend, Emma Kaiser. To a brilliant and booming cohort (all you in the Quad) and the MFAC community of guides, mentors, and good godmothers—Anne Ursu, Meghan Maloney-Vinz, Laura Ruby, Nina LaCour, Laurel Snyder, Marsha Chall, Swati Avasthi, Eliot Schrefer, Coe Booth, Sherri Smith, Brandy Colbert, Meg Medina, Mary Rockcastle, Gene Luen Yang, and so many others.

To new readers, mentors, and sources of support during life after school, Francisco X. Stork, Alison McGhee, Margarita Engle, and Joy Harjo.

To my dream agent Sara Crowe, your keen knowing of how to speak to me and for this book and career. For loving these brothers, for being a force. I'm so happy this path led to you. To those at Pippin Properties, my dream agency, I can't believe your home for me. To Grace Kendall, for being such a champion for this book in all facets. I am absolutely honored to work with you and your brilliance. To the whole dream team at FSG, Trisha Previte, L. Whitt, Ilana Worrell, John Nora, Leigh Ann Higgins, Tatiana Merced-Zarou, Elysse Villalobos, and Elizabeth Lee. To Jazz Aline, for this gorgeous cover.

To my extended family, elders, and relatives—to Aria, to my cousins, Lupe and Tia, who breathed life into magnificent Nicole with me. To my Dakota and Anishinaabe relatives whose ancestral and contemporary land I reside on and whose land is alongside this book. I am ever in debt to you.

To my own beautiful people and family of Talamanca, I am grateful to belong. To my mentor and brother-friend Mainor Ortiz who has passed on our stories and language to me—I am bursting with gratitude and my heart is so full as it beats with our stories.

A deep acknowledgment that Indigenous women in Canada, the United States, and across Latin America are victims of domestic and sexual violence at rates that exceed the general populations. My heart is grateful to MMIW and MMIR for working to support Indigenous survivors and communities and to call for accountability for these crimes.

To my family—my sisters, Jaime and Nikki, and my brother, Kamu. A shout-out to my nephews Isaak and Auston for being my fact-checkers. My dad who has moved on now from this world and my mom—you are the moon and sun that guide me through all seasons. To Lissa and Anna, who aren't family, but gosh it feels like it.

To my love, Grey. Your quiet and daily sacrifices, heart for good, your love and creation of music are all gifts I am ever warmed by. Thank you for valuing art and healing along with me in this life. To your family, which is my family. To our home, my place of peace.

To my sweet little boy who came to the world later in this process. I hope our stories will get to live on in you, and you and others will know there is so much hope even when it feels dark, as told in your namesake.

To God, because without the good and beautiful, I would be lost.

To those I haven't named, I love you dearly.

And lastly, lastly, you, reader. Thank you for your temporal gift, this little piece of your one precious life you chose to spend time reading. I am truly ever grateful.